Showdown at Painted Rock

When mountain man Obadiah Peabody helps out the little wagon train trapped by armed men in Painted Desert, he thinks he is just aiding another bunch of pilgrims aiming for California.

But in among the wagon train sheep there are wolves – the Driscoll brothers, as mean a bunch of owlhoots as a man could wish to meet. After rescuing them, the old mountain man finds himself with a tiger by the tail for the brothers turn on their rescuer and kidnap his adopted granddaughter.

Can Obadiah succeed against seemingly impossible odds? Can he even survive?

Showdown at Painted Rock

WALT MASTERSON

A Black Horse Western

ROBERT HALE · LONDON

© Walt Masterson 2008
First published in Great Britain 2008

ISBN 978-0-7090-8599-7

Robert Hale Limited
Clerkenwell House
Clerkenwell Green
London EC1R 0HT

www.halebooks.com

Typeset by
Derek Doyle & Associates, Shaw Heath
Printed and bound in Great Britain by
CPI Antony Rowe, Wiltshire

*For the nurses and staff at Worthing Hospital
who patched me up when I needed it most.*

CHAPTER ONE

It had been a long, hard chase and the posse had been well led and relentless all the way, so the riders on the tired horses had not had a chance to take a break and rest up. Now they came down out of the hills and faced the shimmering heat of the Painted Desert.

Karl Driscoll was the oldest and the meanest but he was also the most intelligent of the four brothers, so they let themselves be led by him. They didn't like it, but he had kept them alive so far, and none of the other three had any idea what else to do.

'East or west?' asked Lem. He might have made a suggestion himself but it would have led to an argument, and Lem avoided arguments as he avoided all other effort – automatically and on principle.

Donny pulled off his hat and wiped the sweat band with his bandanna. It was a gesture which had become automatic, and his bandanna was almost as wet as the sweat band, but it was better than doing nothing, he thought. Also, it gave him a moment to wait for Karl to make a decision.

Pinkerton was the slim, quick-moving one of the brothers, sudden as a snake and as poisonous. He sat slumped in his saddle and took a moment to pull off his own bandanna. But Pink used it to wipe the action of his Colt and spin the cylinder. He checked the load automatically – and pointlessly, since he already knew he had six shells in the cylinder. His last six. It had been a bloody and hard-fought battle in Hardwick, back down the trail.

And it had, as usual, been Donny's fault. He shot a glance at his brother which would have called for blood from anybody except one of his own family.

It was always Donny's fault. Donny could not keep his hands off a woman, and the one thing guaranteed to get every man in a Western town into his saddle with a Winchester in his hand and blood in his eye was mistreatment of a woman. Pink Driscoll had seen two men hanged for molesting a dancehall girl in one town, and for Pink's money, dancehall girls were only there to be molested.

Still, the girl in Hardwick hadn't been a dancehall girl, just a rancher's daughter in town to do some shopping when she caught Donny's eye. She had been with her mother and a ranch hand to drive their buggy, and they had called at the bank to get some money to buy material for her wedding dress.

And Donny was in the bank at the time. A head of golden hair always caught his eye, and this girl was a beauty by anybody's standards. Right there, in the middle of a hold-up, he had not been able to resist making a grab for the girl.

The ranch hand, there to protect his boss's womenfolk, had grabbed for his gun, but he was a cowboy, not a gunman, and Pink had his Colt out in any case, so the ranch hand died. But in dying he got off one wild shot.

The bullet hit the girl and the bank exploded. The teller produced a shotgun from under the counter; the only other customer, a middle-aged man in range clothes, hit Lem with a chair, and the brothers got out by the skin of their teeth.

In the street a surprisingly energetic sheriff was already running down the sidewalk with his pistol in his hand, and he had time to get off a shot, which struck Karl's shoulder. It was not a fatal wound, nor even a particularly serious one, but it bled a lot, and Karl yelled.

The brothers threw themselves into the saddle and hammered down the street like a full-scale stampede, only to find themselves funnelled into a canyon, which pointed west. Behind them, the town was boiling with men leaping into saddles, and trying to load shotguns at the same time. The dust was already rising, and the pursuit was obviously underway. They had no choice, so west they went, down the canyon, and out the other end.

The pursuit never wavered. Whenever they stopped to rest the horses or fill their canteens, that damned dust cloud appeared on the horizon.

They bound up the flesh wound in Karl's shoulder. When cleaned up with water and his own bandanna it looked painful and bloody but no bones had been hit. Pink, who had the neatest hands, sewed up the gash while Karl's breath hissed between his teeth from the pain. The shock had worn off now, and the bullet wound throbbed painfully.

'Nearly got you,' Donny commented, watching the operation unmoved. Karl shot him a look which should have warned him he was treading the very edge.

'Did the girl die?' he asked between his teeth.

Donny shrugged. 'Hanged if I know,' he said. 'Silly heifer'd be OK now if she'd held still and hadn't screamed. Made that cow-thumper grab for his gun. Her own fault she stopped a bullet.'

For the thousandth time Karl promised himself that if they got out of this one he would make sure Donny lost his interest in women for all time. He had never heard the word 'fratricide' but if he had, he would have had it in his mind right now.

'Doesn't matter whose fault it is,' Lem said, picking his teeth with a thorn. 'We're all to blame, far as them rawhide ranchers is concerned. We best push on.'

Karl hated to admit it, but the fat fool was right. He eased his shirt back over the wound, wincing at the pain.

'So which way do we go, now?' Donny said again.

Behind them to the north was the posse. The dust cloud hadn't caught up yet, but it was still to be seen from time to time, which meant the posse was not far behind them.

To the west, curving south, was the gigantic slash in the earth's crust men were already beginning to call the Grand Canyon. South of the Grand Canyon was Navajo land. The Navajos had been pummelled into a simmering peace by a succession of minor wars which left both them and the white intruders uneasy and untrusting. Go that way, and they would run first into Navajo resentment and then the south curving arm of the Little Colorado. It was a minor obstacle compared with the Canyon, but still a formidable crossing, from what he had heard.

So it had to be south. South into the Painted Desert, now that they had come through what he realized must be the White Mesa. To try to turn east would take them back into the teeth of their pursuers, and into blue-belly land. Fort Defiance was out there somewhere, though he had only a faint idea of where. And by now, the military would have been warned of them and their deeds.

'We go south,' he said. The brothers looked south into the shimmering heat which made the strangely coloured cliffs in the distance look as though they were boiling.

Lem was the first to speak. 'You mean, out there?' he said, huskily. 'In the desert?'

The other two looked just as appalled. Pink

11

opened his mouth to speak, caught Karl's eye and closed it again. Donny bridled, as Karl had known that he would.

'Why do we have to chance our hides out there?' Donny said.

'Because you couldn't keep your hands to your goddamn self!' snarled Karl. He jerked his thumb over his shoulder and winced as the new stitches pulled.

'See that?' he said. They looked and sure enough there was a faint mist of dust on the mesa rim behind them. The pursuit had not let up in three days and nights, and it was not letting up now.

'There's a passel of men back there, each one with a rifle and a rope and one ambition in life: to see us kicking at the end of that rope. It won't be quick and it won't be easy. Them guys ain't let up in three whole days. They been there when we went to sleep and there when we woke up, and so far they ain't guessed wrong once.'

'What you saying?' asked Lem. His brother looked at him with an expression which would have stripped paint.

'That ain't just luck, lunkhead. They got a tracker with them. A Navajo, likely. They can't track at night, on account of he can't see. That's why they ain't caught us up, yet. But they will. There's only four ways to go, north, south, east or west. If we go north or west we'll hit the river, and up here it's deep in the canyons. We might be able to cross ourselves, but we

12

can't get the horses across.

'Go east and we're riding back into them, and the fort's back there someplace. You know where, so we can avoid it? No, nor me neither – so we go south.'

He swung into his saddle. The movement jolted his shoulder and a wave of pain ran through him. The wound seemed hot and he could feel it pulsing. An infection, likely. He would like to get that damned lawman in his sights, just once.

The others started to hurry their horses, and he cursed them into a walk.

'We can see them because they're raising dust. Keep to a walk, we raise less dust, and they should miss it, with luck. Lem, drag a blanket and walk your horse.'

The last was pure spite. Dragging a blanket on this stony ground would shred the blanket and do nothing to obliterate the few tracks they might leave, but he wanted somebody to suffer, and Lem was a good candidate. He'd be too stupid to breathe, if he wasn't told.

With Karl in the lead and Lem dragging his blanket in the rear, the four of them descended into the Painted Desert, where the heat reached hungrily for them. The horses went reluctantly, but they knew better than to balk at the task.

They had managed to fill their canteens overnight, and they were desert-wise enough to give most of it to their mounts, though it had to go sparingly. Karl nagged at Donny when he saw him swigging from his canteen while his horse went thirsty, but he was aware that his own tongue seemed to be twice its normal size and he felt feverish. He began to look for shade where they could stop for a little while.

They found it in a dry wash, with one side steep and throwing shade and the other gentle. If a flash flood should start on the far mountains and funnel down here, they had a relatively easy escape route up on to the desert floor.

Since it was Lem at the rear, it was also Lem who first noticed that the relentless dust cloud had disappeared from their trail. He called Karl's attention to it, and the wounded man nodded tautly at him. Karl was staying in the saddle mainly by an effort of will, with his eyes focused on the horizon.

He made sure the horses had what shade there was and gave his own water by pouring it into his hat and letting the thirsty animal wet its mouth. There was not enough to let it do more, and the men went without their customary coffee even to do this little.

When they were on their way again Pink was riding point. The day seemed endless, and men and animals were at the end of their tether as the desert afternoon started its startlingly sudden descent into night.

Pink suddenly pulled up his horse, and waved his brothers down. They stopped obediently, and waited while he dismounted and bellied up to the low ridge in front. He was there for a few minutes, then he came back down to them.

'Fire up ahead,' he said. 'Only one, and it's small, looks like a campfire. Want to chance it?'

Karl swore bitterly. A fire might mean the posse had somehow got ahead of them. If so, would it be aware that they were coming along from the north? He shook his head and forced himself to think carefully.

It could not be the posse. The brothers had come in as straight a line as the terrain would let them; to get so far ahead the posse would have had to have grown wings. In any case, men waiting to ambush the fugitives would scarcely light a fire, which would warn them.

'Ain't the law,' he concluded. 'More like pilgrims we just happen to have come across. They'll have water, food too. We go on down, but go careful. Pink, keep a rein on your temper, and Don, if there's a woman there and you so much as look at her crooked I swear I'll kill you myself. Slowly.'

His brothers knew him well enough not to take the warnings lightly. In single file they rode their tired horses down from the ridge and approached the fire.

CHAPTER TWO

Karl was bothered by the wound in his arm, so for a fateful few moments he did not see the danger he was leading his brothers into.

Like any other Westerners, he knew the rules for approaching a stranger's camp in the dark. The brothers made noise as they approached out of the night, and when they were still outside the camp he rose in his stirrups and called: 'Hello, the camp!'

There was some hurried movement among the shadowy figures around the fire, then a voice called: 'Who's out there?'

'Four travellers lookin' for a fire and maybe some coffee,' Karl shouted.

'Coffee we got,' said the unseen camp spokesman. 'Come ahead but keep your hands where we can see 'em!'

Hands empty and in sight, they edged the horses slowly into the camp. There were two wagons, drawn up side by side, with a cooking fire in the space between them. Some horses were picketed on a line alongside them. At one end of the line a shadowy figure sat shapelessly by a rock. Firelight glinted on a rifle barrel pointed in their direction.

By the nearest wagon a bearlike figure turned into a man with a blanket wrapped round his shoulders as the flames picked him out. He, too, had a gun in his hands. It was a shotgun, Karl noticed, and the barrels followed their progress.

Carefully, they dismounted and tied their horses to the end of the picket line. Then, one by one, they stepped into the firelight and took off their hats.

There were women there, Karl saw with a stab of misgiving, and, from her outline, at least one of them was young. He shot a glance at Donny, but his brother had already noticed her.

'Howdy, folks,' Karl said. 'No need for nerves, now. We're just four men on the road, saw your fire. Surely appreciate some of that good coffee you folks are brewing there.'

The people round the fire made room for them, and one of the women handed them tin cups while another filled them with coffee. It was scalding, and Lem swore hastily as he burned his lips on the rim of the cup. Karl, more careful, wrapped gloved hands round the cup and blew on it. The smell was strong and delicious.

'You folks making south?' he asked, sipping cautiously. One of the men grunted at him. The rest of the people stayed silent. There was a tension

17

around the fire he did not understand, and he revised his plans. There must be no violence. These people were far too careful to be taken by surprise, and he had already seen at least two shotguns pointed in his direction.

By the time he had finished the coffee he had learned that they were following the old Mormon trail down to the crossing and were then planning on striking west and down to Yuma to cross the Colorado there. Nobody mentioned whether they were in fact Mormons themselves, which probably meant that they were not.

They expected to camp the following night at Painted Rock, which they estimated was about thirty to forty miles down the trail. The distance was pretty ambitious for slow-moving wagons but, unless they ran into any kind of trouble, was achievable.

Karl's attention was caught by a movement at the edge of the firelight, and he glanced up, his hand reaching instinctively for his gun. The gesture was noticed by the group's leader, a thickset middle-aged man called Paulus, and though he did nothing about it, his attitude changed. From that moment onwards he did not trust the brothers, and Karl knew it.

He also knew that if he had tried to draw his Colt, he would by now be dead. As his hand fell on the butt he heard quite clearly, out in the darkness, the sound of two guns being cocked, one of which was behind him.

Pinkerton noticed it, too. Donny and Lem did not.

The conversation round the fire died into silence.

And into it stepped one of the most beautiful girls Karl had ever seen.

She was tall and willowy and her hair was burnished gold which picked up the rich glow of the firelight. Her face was heart-shaped, her lips full and her nose short. Even in the firelight he could see that she had large eyes and long lashes.

Donny, he knew without looking, was transfixed. If ever a girl had been designed for him, this was she. Even Lem, usually conscious of nothing he could not eat, drink or steal, was frozen into place.

The girl stood in the glow and looked around the ring of faces.

'Visitors!' she said delightedly. 'Why didn't you tell me, Pa? I love visitors, and we never have any on the trail. Hello there, boys. I'm Betty Paulus. Who are you?'

Karl had a nightmare feeling that he was being swept along on a tide he could not control. Donny was reaching over the fire to shake her hand, Lem was wiping his hand on the front of his shirt so that he could do the same, and only Pink remained apparently unmoved. He stayed where he was on his log, still sipping coffee from the tin mug, eyes watchful over the rim. He looked as though he was coiled, ready to strike.

The tension was broken by Paulus. The thickset man stood up, tossed the dregs of his coffee on the fire, and threw the cup into a bucket they were using to wash up.

19

'My daughter, Betty,' he said. 'Bet, these gentle-men are on their way south and we offered them the courtesy of our fire. They can camp with us tonight, if they've a mind to?' He turned the statement into a question by turning towards Karl, who nodded.

'Mighty neighbourly of you, Mr Paulus,' he said. 'Glad to take your hospitality for the night.' He noticed they were not being offered food, and wondered why not.

They were given a space within the wagon enclosure. The migrants, he noticed, slept under their wagons with the womenfolk inside. Laid out by the fire, the Driscoll brothers were illuminated by the glow and surrounded by their hosts. There were ten men in the migrant party, Karl estimated, and six women.

At no time was he able to see more than six of the men in full view, which means there were four out of sight, and he had the strong feeling they were watch-ing him and his brothers with a steady gaze.

As full night closed in and the sounds of the camp died away, he could hear the horses in the picket line crunching steadily on their feed, the occasional stamp of a hoof. Out beyond the dying firelight there was an occasional sound as one of the sentries moved around. There were at least two out there that he could hear, one near the horses and the other at the open ends of the camp horseshoe. He wondered where the other two were.

He lay on his back, his head on his saddle as a

pillow and watched the fire die down into glowing coals. Out beyond the wagons he could see the mountains outlined, black against a curtain of stars so bright they could have been lanterns. The moon was high and full, and silvered the scenery dramatically.

He stiffened when he looked at the black looming profile of the mountains. High on the side of the nearest one, a jagged peak with sloping shoulders, a pinprick of light flickered for a moment.

Tense now, he shifted his focus and saw it again. A fire, flickering in the heights, and just exposed for a split second. Perhaps a man had passed in front of it, covering the fire for a moment. He stared at the spot for a long time, but did not see it again.

Disturbed, he sat up and began to get out of his blankets, but a voice from the dark behind him told him to stay still.

'But there's a fire up there on the heights,' he said.

'I seen it. Go back to sleep,' said the sentry. Karl lay down, watching the mountain. Eventually he fell asleep still waiting for it to reappear.

The camp was astir when he awakened the next morning; fires had been lit and bacon was frying. He and his brothers packed their blanket rolls and accepted a bucket of water to wash in. There was no soap, and after they had used the water he noticed a boy took it to the horses.

21

'Nothing wasted,' said Paulus, shouldering past with his blanket roll. He dropped it over the tailgate of one of the wagons, and turned to help one of the other men with the horse teams.

There were two teams of draught animals, good stock in good condition, and the harness was good quality and well looked after. The men put the teams into the harness easily and expertly and the horses were well trained enough to do what they were required to do without fuss.

There were four saddle animals with the party, but as soon as their riders climbed aboard they rode off beyond the road and vanished into a fold in the ground. Five minutes later they reappeared with a small herd of horses and fell into line behind the wagons, which were already moving. Together, the wagons and horses represented quite an investment, and Karl found himself reassessing the value of the party. There was money here, real money.

He glanced up to see Paulus watching him from the other side of the lead wagon. The man gave the order to get the little caravan under way, and the horses fell in behind the wagons, with one of the men riding drag and an outrider on each side of the trail.

Karl led his brothers off to one side, where they were not riding in the dust, and Lem ranged his horse alongside. He was watching the wagon master's pretty daughter, who was driving the lead wagon. Karl noticed that she might look willowy but she handled the four-horse team as well as any stage driver. The foot which was operating the brake lever was booted and there was the leg of a pair of jeans showing under the skirt.

There were no hold-ups on the way to Painted Rock so their progress was surprisingly smooth.

Paulus included them in the midday meal, which was taken on the move. One of the boys rode out to them with a pot full of coffee and a box of biscuits which must have been cooked last night against the day's need. They were good, and there was some cheese to keep them company.

But the four men were not invited into the column of march, and Karl wondered even more.

He had expected the normal kind of pilgrim on the trail, tough from their journey so far, but trusting of him and his brothers because they were white and armed and knew their way around.

Lem spat at a lizard on a rock beside the trail and asked: 'What now? If we're going to take 'em we'll have to be quick. Be in Painted Rock by sundown at this rate.'

Karl glanced at him through narrowed eyes. 'Leave 'em alone, Lem,' he said. 'We got enough troubles the way things are. Painted Rock ain't so far down, and the way I hear it, they got no sheriff at the moment. Anything we want to do, we can do there, or after there. This side just leave 'em alone.'

Lem shrugged, but his eyes were on the blonde wagon driver, and his thoughts were not hard to read.

Karl twisted on his saddle to look at their back trail. For the first time for days, it was clear. No cloud of dust. No sign of pursuit. Had the posse given up? He didn't read them that way, but sooner or later despair must take the edge off the desire for pursuit. Maybe that had happened now.

There was a call from the eastern side of the trail and he watched while a single rider came in on the caravan. He was a young man in a slouch hat, and he rode with a long-barrelled rifle balanced across his saddle horn.

The column seemed to be expecting him, and the men gathered around him as he ranged alongside the lead wagon. Paulus joined the group and for the first time in the day the wagons came to a standstill. The men sat their horses and the newcomer talked to them. What he said apparently surprised them.

Karl was curious and wary. The news brought by the boy on the rangy horse seemed to bring about some excitement in the group. Guns were checked and even the pretty Betty produced a short-barrelled Greener shotgun from under her wagon seat and checked the loads.

One of the men said something to Paulus and pointed at Karl and his brothers. Paulus looked over in their direction and cantered over to them. The brothers bunched up as he arrived, raising dust and looking troubled.

'Got some bad news,' Paulus said. 'Don't affect you boys, but you should be aware of it. There's some

24

men coming up behind and there may be trouble. If you don't want to be caught up in a fight that's not of your making, nobody will think any less of you if you ride away.'

'What kind of trouble?' said Lem, glancing over his shoulder at the hills.

'Not your trouble. Not your business. Was I you, I'd ride on and forget I ever seen this wagon train. Stay, and you may get caught up in shooting. But if you stay, you'd maybe be better off with the rest of us. Come on in.' He turned his horse and cantered away.

'Dust coming!' Pink said right off. He had been watching their back trail, and so was the first to notice the signs. The others followed his pointing hand. Lem cursed viciously.

'Damn posse!' he spat. Karl shook his head.

'Ain't our lot,' he said. 'They'd be coming down from north-east, and this lot's coming in from the west.'

Donny was all for staying. He could not get the beautiful Betty off his mind, and his very enthusiasm for staying made Karl want to shoot him for a fool. But the general feeling was to stay. Reluctantly, Karl gave the order to ride in to the wagons, and the four cantered over to the trail where the wagons had got under way again, and lined up behind them.

The youngest of the boys was riding drag with the horses, and he acknowledged them with a wave of the hand. He had his rifle laid across his knees, and under the tattered hat what looked like a cheroot

25

stuck out of his mouth. They had got closer before Karl realized it was a short length of stick. The boy was cleaning his teeth.

Karl and Pink ranged alongside the boy and Karl sent Donny and Lem up to the head of the little column, where Paulus and two of the other men were leading. Donny tipped his hat to Betty on her driving seat as he went past. She grinned at him and waved her whip.

'How long do you reckon?' said the horse-herder, glancing over his shoulder at the approaching dust. Karl looked back at it and shrugged.

'Hour, maybe. They're coming along right smartly,' he said. 'Know who they are?'

The boy glanced at him, surprised.

'Didn't Mr Paulus tell you?' he said. 'They're from back beyond Lee's Crossing. We had trouble with them coming down, and some shots was fired. Man got killed, and they blamed us. That there's a hanging mob and they say they're going to hang one of us for the killing.'

Karl looked at him. 'Did you kill him?'

The boy shook his head. 'Nope. One of his own people did, trying to kill Mr Paulus. He threw a knife, and Mr Paulus, why, he just ducked his head, and the knife went into the heart of this man who was on their own side. Thought we'd thrown 'em when we come across the Crossing, but it looks like they're dead set on a hanging.'

'Will they get one?'

The boy shot him a glance filled with contempt. 'Only if they decide to hang one of their own,' he said. 'Us'uns ain't that keen on being hung.'

He chirruped to his horse and went off like a greyhound to head off a mustang with a lust for travel, heading it back into the remuda and pushing the herd faster in the tracks of the wagons.

Karl had been keeping his eye on the pursuing dust cloud and he knew they could not outrun it without abandoning the wagons. For a moment he considered riding off now and relying on the pursuers being too busy with the Paulus party to pursue them. But another look at the following cloud and he knew he had left it too late. Paulus's fate was also theirs. He wheeled his horse and rode back a way to get a better view.

When he got his telescope focused he wished he had not. The pursuing posse was huge: around twenty men from what he could see through their dust. They were pushing their horses hard, and he saw more than one stumble in the dust. Tired animals ridden by savage men. He had seen lynch mobs before, and he was looking at one now.

Paulus rode up beside him as he was folding the telescope, and put a hand out for it. Karl gave it to him.

'Whoever they are, they're bound and determined,' he said, as the older man stared through the glass.

'They're Mormon-haters', Paulus said. 'Men like

27

them done for more innocent travellers than the Cheyenne. Bigots, murderers and thieves.'

Karl was genuinely surprised. 'You Mormons?' he said. 'Ain't seen nothing to show it.'

Paulus shut the telescope and handed it back.

'We ain't,' he said. 'Got nothing against them myself. Man wants to believe in a book written on metal plates and dictated by an angel nobody seen, that's his business. But the truth is that those men coming down like the hounds of hell was on their tails are just road bandits with minds like rabid skunks, and they're after my family.'

He swung his horse and rode after the wagons which were trundling along at a fair old pace. The horses could not keep up this speed for long, and still live, but the urge to flee was strong in the drivers, and they had little to lose by exhausting their animals.

Karl followed Paulus, and changed his mind about fleeing. The men in that oversized posse would follow him anyway, and his best hope for survival was to add his firepower to that of the Paulus group and see how it all came out.

He was actually joining the wagons when Paulus pulled alongside Betty's wagon and shouted to her to pull off the road towards a rampart of rocks to the east. They stood like a stone fence along the foot of towering cliffs, and the wagons, lurching and bumping, made for them.

Pink was already there. He stood up on one of the

rocks, waving the wagons towards the southern end of the pile, and they swung south, then curled in behind the natural rampart. The outriders drove the horses after them, and Karl and his other brothers followed them in.

Behind the rocks was a kind of natural corral, open on the southern end, closed off as high as a mounted man by a natural barricade of rocks round the foot of the cliff. Above it the cliff face itself curled over like a breaking wave. The wagons fitted neatly on the detritus slope under the overhang. So long as nobody got round that southern end, it made a fortress.

They pulled up and dismounted. Pink was already standing sentry on one of the rocks, watching the approaching riders. Donny had managed to get himself in among the womenfolk, Lem was tucked into a vantage point, his jaws moving rhythmically. Karl wondered irrelevantly where in this desert landscape he had found something to chew on.

Armed, dug in like a beleaguered garrison, and now surrounded, they waited for the arrival of their enemies.

CHAPTER THREE

The riders slowed in their tracks when they realized what they were now up against, and a couple of warning shots in front of their horses' hoofs brought them up short. They sat just out of range, talking between themselves, and eventually walked their horses forward again. This time one man rode further than the rest until another warning shot in front of his horse stopped him.

He dismounted and walked a few paces until he judged he was within earshot, then cupped his hands round his mouth.

'Come out!' he called. 'We just want to talk to you.'

'Yeah,' shouted Paulus. 'You can talk all you want from there. We hear you.'

'We are a legally deputized posse from Lee's Crossing. You got no business shooting on us. All we want is the murderer of our friend. Rest of you can go free.'

'Damned good of him,' grunted Paulus. 'We're

free now. Keep an eye on those others, will you? They're trying to sidle up while we talk.'

'You hear me?' the man shouted. He was not a reassuring sight. A tattered hat hung its drooping brim around his ears. His hair was long and looked greasy, and his duster coat flapped around his ankles with the wind from the desert. He had a drooping moustache hanging over the corners of his mouth. He looked as though he smelled.

'You folks ready to die to protect one man? Don't be fools. We got you trapped there, and if we have to come in and get him, no telling what will happen to the rest of you. Could get right nasty! You got womenfolks in there you need to think about.'

Paulus spat on his hands and raised the extra rear sight on his rifle to give him greater accuracy. The rifle was a Winchester '73 and had seen some use. Paulus did not look like a man used to missing his aim.

'You finished? Then I got a question for you, mister,' he called.

'Yeah?' the sneer was audible in the tone. 'And what would that be, Mormon?'

Paulus cuddled the rifle into his shoulder and leaned forward slightly over the rock.

'How you going to get back to your pack, you running dog? You left your horse way too far back for a fast start!'

The man laughed mockingly, and spread out his hands as though trying to make himself into a bigger target.

31

'Everybody knows Mormons can't kill, just like they know Mormon women sleep with anybody. How many women you got in your wagon, mister ? They'll be glad to see a real man, by and by!'

'Won't be you, though,' said Donny from the next rock, and his first shot took the spokesman cleanly through the shirt pocket. Paulus looked back at him, startled by the shot, just in time to see Karl pick off the man holding the loose horse, a good hundred yards further back. Prompted by the outbreak of shooting, Pink fired from further along the barricade and also scored a hit. His target was already moving, though, and almost fell out of the saddle, but retained enough strength to grab his saddle horn, and stay on his horse.

'*Down!*' roared Paulus, and the men who were spread out along the barricade threw themselves on to their faces as the posse overcame its surprise and fired back. Bullets spattered into the rocks and one or two whined off the overhang and fell into the safe area where the wagons were. The women leaped from the wagon boxes and crawled under them. More than one, Karl noticed, was dragging a shotgun with her. This was turning into a formidable bunch of people.

Once the first fusillade had been fired – and the range was extreme, so the bullets which came into the shelter were erratically aimed – the posse pulled back well out of range, and bunched together. They seemed to be talking, and Karl knew just what they were doing. Planning trouble.

Paulus slid down behind his rock and turned a furious face on Donny. 'What you think you're doing, firing like that?' he roared. 'Next time you wait for my order before you fire!'

Donny looked at him, unmoved. 'What you got your long johns in a twist about, mister?' he said, contemptuously. 'That *hombre* was threatening your folk and threatening to abuse your womenfolk. Kill him and there's one less. What can they do to us in here? Nothing. Now, there's three less of them and no less of us.'

Karl silently agreed with him. If this bunch had followed them all the way down from the Crossing, they were not going to turn round and ride off, just because the wagon boss told them to. They were after revenge, loot and women in that order. And the wagon party offered all three. If they could be induced to give themselves up without a fight, so much the better.

But he could not afford to antagonize Paulus at this time. The man had to be kept sweet so they could shelter in his wagon train.

'No harm done, Mr Paulus,' he growled. 'Them 'uns is just after your womenfolk anyway. No getting them off and sending them home with their tails between their legs. Might as well kill as many as possible right from the start. Fewer to shoot back at us later.'

One of the boys called a warning from down at the

open end of their fortress. The rattle of racing horses' hoofs and a barrage of shots from their front warned them there was a diversionary tactic going on. Karl poked his rifle over the parapet and started shooting at racing forms on dusty horses outside the barrier.

The attack lasted a surprisingly short time, and withdrew in its own dust cloud, leaving two dead horses and one dead man outside the barricade. Another man was sprawled on the ground, but as they looked at him, he suddenly came to life, sprang to his feet with surprising agility and raced for the open country.

'Let him go!' bawled Paulus, but Pink Driscoll picked him off with a round between the shoulder blades and he cartwheeled before landing on his face. He made no more attempts to rise.

Paulus was furious. 'Why do that? He couldn't do no harm to us!'

Pink ignored him, reloading his carbine while he watched the posse as it milled about out of range. The men out there were plainly hatching something. Karl dug out his telescope again and tried to see more detail.

'What they doing?' asked Paulus anxiously. Karl got the telescope steadied against a boulder and focused carefully. It did not help a great deal, except that he could see the men out there dividing into two groups. At the centre of each group was a man carrying something on his saddle horn, and as he watched, the two groups began to move, circling wide to stay out of range until they both turned at the same moment and raced for the rock barricade.

'Somebody in the middle of each bunch they're tryin' to protect,' he offered. 'Dunno why, but it can't be good for us. Try to get the man in the middle. He's carrying something, and they want him to get it here.'

The two groups were travelling fast and on a curving approach. One was aiming for the end of the barricade to the south, where the natural gate provided a weak spot. The other came straight for the rocks. They were crouched over their horses' necks, and they had the look of a determined bunch.

All the men were firing now, a running barrage of lead. One by one, members of the charging posse were being picked off, but not enough to stop them, and never the two men carrying what looked like packages. They seemed to bear some kind of supernatural protection. Even Karl could feel the hair on the back of his neck pricking as he fired and fired again, seemingly without effect.

The two groups were close to the rocks now. Another man was slapped out of the saddle as though he had been swatted by some invisible fly whisk, but the group opened up and the men carrying the packages swerved and rode along the foot of the barrier. The man in the frontal attack lobbed his package and Karl saw a tiny trail of smoke coming from it as it arced towards the rocks.

'Dynamite!' he bawled, hurling himself into the

space between two boulders. One of the boys was already there, and Karl dragged him out of the refuge and hurled himself in, just as the package exploded, low above the barrier. The boy he had evicted from the cleft gave a hiccoughing cry and fell down the inside of the rock barrier.

The second bomber had swung south towards the open end of the refuge. Bullets screamed off the rocks near him but he galloped on, unhurt, and threw his bomb on an arc which was plainly going to take it into the refuge where the women and youngsters cowered beneath the wagons. In that confined space, it would have devastating effect.

But as all eyes followed it there was a shot which boomed out louder than the spiteful crack of the Winchesters and Colts. The bomb exploded harmlessly outside the barrier before it had cleared the rocks, and one of the riders following the bombthrower was blasted out of his saddle. His horse, squealing piteously, was smashed down by the explosion. The rider simply disappeared. Later, while they cleared up, they were continually finding him.

As the accompanying riders withdrew the defenders poured a raking fire into them. They had come too close, certain that their bombs would disable the defenders, and now they paid the price. Vengeful men who were good shots and had just seen their families threatened with obliteration, fired as fast as they could work the loading levers, and the effect was devastating.

When the surviving members of the fake posse grouped safely outside the Winchesters' range they represented no more than a third of the men who had come riding down the trail, eager for loot and revenge.

There was plainly some sort of argument going on out there. Even at this range Karl could see arms being waved, and they could all hear faint shouting. Eventually, one side seemed to prevail, and the posse spread out and started a slow, measured advance to the barrier.

Karl checked on his brothers and found them checking on him. All were unharmed. He was disappointed to see that Donny was unmarked, and firmly embedded in the defences between Betty and a teenage boy.

A groan came from the foot of the barrier, and one of the women ran over to see who it was. She gave a sharp cry of dismay, but at that moment shooting started from outside the barrier, and Karl switched his attention.

The approaching line of horsemen had stopped, dismounted and started shooting at the barrier. They had left their horses back out of range and crawled closer, well hidden in the stones and straggling brush.

Bullets started to scream inside the overhang, ricocheting off the curving roof of the recess, and smacking into the rocks within. They made an ugly sound, and once Karl had worked out what the remaining members of the posse were about, he realized that the posse members were deliberately bouncing bullets off the ceiling behind the barrier.

He had seen ricochet wounds before. The big lead slugs were flattened and deformed by the impact on the rock, and made hideous wounds. It was only a matter of time before these bullets found a mark. The Spanish conquistadors, he recalled, had used the technique against Navajos up in the Canyon de Chelly, and wiped out a group sheltering on a ledge which the Spanish could not hit directly.

As he began to slide out of his hidy-hole one of the draught horses screamed and went down, thrashing around with its legs. One of the women put her carbine to its head and put it out of its agony. The barrage intensified.

But even as it did so he heard, quite clear above the sharper reports, the same deep boom he had heard before during the grenade attack. Out in the desert somebody screamed. There was confused shouting.

Another boom, another yell and suddenly the men on the barricade were shooting furiously again.

He hooked his elbows over the rock and looked out, cautiously. Out on the flats the men who had been sniping were running furiously for their horses, jinking and ducking.

Even as Karl watched the new gun boomed out again, and one of the running men collapsed in a shapeless heap. The report seemed to come from

38

behind him and above, and he looked upwards and wondered.

The remainder of the running men got to their horses, and hurled themselves into the saddle. As they did so, the unseen gun boomed again and one of the horsemen was thrown off his mount as though he had been kicked in the head. He did not get up again, but the rest of the posse rode like demons.

There were pitifully few survivors. Of the score or so men who had come hammering down the trail, he counted only four riding away. The anonymous shooter above him stopped firing, presumably because the targets were out of range even for his remarkable weapon, and the remaining bandits disappeared towards the old Mormon road and home.

Karl jumped down from the barrier to find two women bending over the teenager he had evicted from his hiding-place. The lad had fallen fifteen feet or so, and his ankle was swelling even as they got his boot off. Broken or sprained, it was plainly out of commission and the boy was in pain.

As Karl came down off the rocks, their eyes met. The boy opened his mouth to complain, and Karl bent over him solicitously.

'Gee, I'm sorry about that, kid,' he said seriously. 'I had to get you out of the line of fire somehow, and there wasn't no time to do nothing else.'

The boy looked baffled. 'But I wasn't in the line of fire,' he protested. 'I was safe in the hole in the rocks.

You pulled me out!'

Karl looked up to see the women staring at him accusingly. Paulus came down from his rock vantage point and leaned over the lad. He felt the ankle, and though the lad did not cry out, his body stiffened and the colour went from his face.

'Not broken, I think,' Paulus opined. 'But a bad sprain. Bind it up and try to keep the bandages cool. There may be a medico in Painted Rock. We'll be there by dark, I think. Maybe.'

He obviously didn't believe it himself, and Karl caught the expression on the faces of the other people. They were all looking at him, and their expressions were not friendly.

Karl was not a coward. But every one of the adults in the party had a gun in his or her hand. The women mainly had shotguns. The four brothers were pretty well surrounded.

He caught the expression in Pink's eye and stepped over smoothly to stand in front of him. His brother was hell on wheels with a gun, but in a situation like this speed was not as important as sheer numbers. If shooting started, the brothers had no chance of winning. They might take a few with them, but they would die here.

'Now, see here, folks,' he started easily. 'Young feller here's hurt and confused. We both dove for that crack at the same time, and we collided. I'm mortal sorry he's hurt, but if I hadn't knocked him down, he'd have stopped a slug for sure.'

He looked round. The faces looked uncompromising. They did not believe him, and he eased his hand back closer to his gun. He was damned if a bunch of sodbuster migrants were going to pull one over on him or his brothers, even if he did need them to get to Painted Rock.

For a moment, he thought they would rush him. Then a new voice broke the tension, and they were all caught unawares.

'Hold hard, there, horse!' said a voice which seemed to come from a man's very boots. 'Don't go pulling no iron on the man just saved all your hides!'

All the heads turned to the open end of their fortress, to find it was occupied by a scarecrow figure who seemed to come from the past. A long, long way into the past.

The horse was the first wonder. Karl was a good judge of horseflesh: there had been times when his life depended on his ability to pick a fast runner with bottom which would keep it going after other mounts had blown and foundered. But he had never in his life seen a horse as ugly as this one.

It was a bilious colour of yellow, with a hammer head and sloping back. It was knock-kneed and had an evil look about the eye. When it whickered, it showed a mouth full of teeth like yellowed tombstones.

Its rider was no better. He was an old man, dressed in very old and stained buckskins which looked as though they were older than their wearer, and certainly carried traces of him spread about the front. He was evidently a messy eater, and the signs of it showed.

On his head there was a hat which had once been black, with a wide, flat brim and a domed top. From the shadow under the brim peered a bearded face with beady, dark eyes and and a thin-lipped mouth which showed a ragged picket fence of teeth when he smiled.

He was smiling now. In his right hand, with its butt resting on his right thigh, was a rifle so long it looked like a museum piece. In contrast to its owner, it was polished and as clean as when it left the gunsmith's workshop. The dark wood of the butt and forepiece gleamed as though it had been recently oiled and the brasswork which capped the butt and framed the action would have made a rifle company sergeant-major weep with delight.

He rode a worn black saddle behind which were two thick saddle-bags, and his feet, which were tucked into his high stirrups, were in moccasins rather than boots, the high-legged moccasins favoured by the Apache and the other desert tribes. From the top of the right one protruded the polished brass pommel of a knife.

'You folks fixing to go far?' he said, his little black eyes ranging over the staring faces. 'If so, was I you, I'd be on my way. There's Apaches not too far to your north, and I seen another passel of white men making their way down from the river. Ain't going to be too healthy round here, give it a short while.'

Paulus was the first to get his voice back,

'That the rifle I heard during the fight?' he asked.

The old man laughed. Compared with his grave-yard voice, his laugh was surprisingly high-pitched and more like a giggle.

'Weren't no other,' he croaked. 'Old Betsy, she got one hell of a voice, ain't she, horse? One hell of a voice!'

'We're right obliged to you. You turned the tide of the battle for us,' Paulus said. 'Won't you tell us your name, mister. . . ?'

'Peabody, horse. Obadiah Peabody. Pleased to make your acquaintance, I'm sure. You sure are dead right about that there fracas, though. For a bunch of rats like yonder, you sure do need a rifle like Betsy. Got a deep voice, and a long reach, has Betsy. Load my own shells and cast my own bullets. That way I know how far she'll reach. Pays to know that, it do.'

His eye strayed round the makeshift fort.

'With women and kids, I'd recommend you just get going, horse,' he added. 'I ain't just calculating about them Apaches. I been following them a couple of days. Seen the other party of white, back along the trail, too. They're all coming along kind of slow, but they're moving and you ain't. Bound to catch up sooner or later. Sooner's the way I calculate.'

CHAPTER FOUR

They buried the dead of the shoot-out in a large hole and put a marker over them. Paulus was all for holding a service, but he caught the beady eye of Obadiah Peabody upon him and changed his mind, merely consigning their souls to their God.

'If God's listening, he'll know what you want to say. If he ain't, then ain't no point in saying it,' opined Peabody, and he pointed his rifle one-handed at the trail.

'Do you folks make your time down the trail. I'll scout around a mite. Don't fret none if you don't see me. I'll find you. Got about two more hours of daylight, I calculate. Take you most of the way to Painted Rock. I'll see you the rest of the way.'

He turned the horse, and trotted it away towards the cliffs, and after a few hundred yards was invisible. The watching migrants gave a collective blink, then turned their attention back to the trail.

Karl gave their back-trail a good deal of attention

44

as the afternoon wore on, but saw no tell-tale dust. That reassured him about the second party of white men, who were, he was pretty certain, the posse. But he admitted to himself if to nobody else that Apaches unsettled him.

'They don't cheer nobody up,' Paulus said drily when Karl mentioned it in an attempt to speed up the pace of the march. 'If we could go faster, we'd be doing it.'

He turned away, but Karl noticed that he did in fact have a word with the women who were driving the wagons, and the pace did in fact improve. They were hampered by the fact that one wagon had been reduced to a team of three, and it unbalanced the dead horse's former harness mate. But they managed a respectable speed none the less.

After the first hour and a half, at a much improved pace, Paulus started looking for a campsite. The sun had started its descent to the western horizon, a jagged collection of peaks, and the remaining daylight was slowly dying.

Karl was divided. Like the settlers, he wanted to get to the comparative security of the town: unlike them, he was not looking forward to being caught up by the white posse who, he figured, would also be aiming for it.

But just as Paulus raised his hand above his head to sign a stop, Obadiah Peabody appeared next to the lead wagon as though he had grown in an instant out of the desert. The horse was covered in dust, and

Peabody's clothes had been reduced to the dun shade of the land, but Betsy, his rifle, still gleamed like a precious stone.

'Don't hold up, here, horse!' Peabody called to Paulus. 'Keep 'em rolling, and you'll eat your dinner in the Painted Rock!'

The women shook out the traces and even the horses seemed to recognize that the trail was almost over, and threw themselves into their collars with renewed strength. They hauled the wagons up a gentle slope in the trail and as they topped it, first one and then another light popped out of the gathering dusk in front of them.

They were at Painted Rock.

The wagons rolled into the main street of the tiny settlement as full dark fell. The darkness was kind to the little town. In the glow of the oil lamps outside the saloon and along the boardwalk, the boarded fronts of the buildings took on a warm colour, and the canvas roofs which covered several of the newer buildings faded into the dark.

Paulus pulled the wagons to a standstill and called to one of the men who had come on to the sidewalk to watch the wagons roll in.

'Where's the best place to camp?' he said. The man grinned a gap-toothed grin.

'California's well spoke of,' he chuckled. 'Tucson's good. An' they think well of Phoenix. Take your pick.'

The hangers-on giggled like schoolgirls, but

Paulus was an experienced trail boss, and met much the same reception at every new town. He took off his hat and wiped the sweat band with his bandanna while he waited for the laughter to stop.

'Any place better round here than any other to make camp?' he tried.

'Sure is,' said the town wit and was about to expand on the statement when even in the light of the lanterns, he saw a certain light in Paulus's eye which said 'enough'.

'Keep down to the end of the street, and there's a livery and a couple of corrals on your right. You can put your stock in there, and camp alongside, long as you're careful about your fires. We don't want the town burned down – only just got her up!'

That got him another laugh, but their hearts weren't in it, and the hitching rail leaners started to fade back into the saloon.

Paulus walked the wagons along to the corral indicated, and found they had been directed properly. There was a livery stable there, as well as the corrals. An old man in worn jeans with his braces over his red union suit shoulders sat on a barrel on the boardwalk and smoked a corncob pipe.

'You folks need stables for the night?' he asked in a reedy voice. Paulus opted for the corrals and a hay feed for their livestock, and was directed to a stretch of land beyond the corrals, where piles of stones and ashes indicated more than one caravan had passed through. They drew the wagons up in their usual

47

night-time formation, and the women started fires while the men saw to the stock.

Karl and his brothers made for the saloon, after a curiously muted parting from their travelling companions. Peabody went with them, and Karl noticed he was greeted with affection by the locals. The old man hitched his ugly horse to the rail outside the saloon, and took his rifle inside with him.

Ranged along the bar, the brothers ordered drinks and looked around. The saloon was surprisingly full for the size of the town. Men ate and drank, and from a rear room came the sound of a guitar being played. A woman's voice was singing something low and sweet, and on an impulse, Karl took his beer and wandered to the arch which marked the division between the front and back rooms.

The singer was a handsome, dark woman who was accompanying herself on a guitar. She sat against the rear wall of the place, on a small raised platform which also had a piano on it.

The rest of the room was taken up with tables and chairs, and a man in a long white apron was serving food. He glanced up at Karl and nodded.

'Howdy, mister! You fixing to eat tonight? We got beef and chilli,' he said. Karl nodded and the waiter, hands full of plates, pointed his chin at a table against the wall.

'Set and I'll serve you!' he called, and backed through a swing door releasing into the room the clamour of voices and the smell of beef on a griddle.

Karl sat, called over his shoulder to the men at the bar, and they walked over to join him. Donny's eye fell predictably on the singer, and a long, slow grin started to spread across his face. Inwardly, Karl groaned. They were off again.

The meal when it came was surprisingly good. It was, of course, beef, but it was tender and bloody and the beans with it were tasty with chilli and garlic. The brothers ate well, but Donny never took his eyes off the singer.

Karl watched her, too. She was not a conventional beauty, but there was a serenity about her which first attracted and then fascinated. Her dark hair was long and straight and looked like cascading silk. Her eyes were large and soft and her lips had a sweetness which complemented her excellent voice.

He found himself staring at her hands, too. They were graceful and sure on the strings of the instrument, and they called a purity of music from the guitar that he had rarely heard before.

Lem watched her for a while while he shovelled steak down his throat, and when she came to a break in the music, he belched loudly and laughed.

The girl looked at him with her disgust written plain on her face. The men who had been listening to her all reacted the same way. There were rumbles of annoyance all round the room, and one man said, clearly: 'Sorry about the wildlife, ma'am!'

Lem was on his feet instantly, looking round the dining room with blood in his eye.

'Who said that?' he snarled. 'Who the goddamned hell said that?'

There was a silence, but he could see the mockery on the faces of the men in the room. He glared round, and everywhere his eye fell he saw only sneers and contempt.

One man, a young cowhand from the look of him, was still eating and, in the sudden silence, his knife and fork made clicking noises on the plate.

'You!' shouted Lem, pointing at him. 'You say that?'

The young man ignored him and went on eating. He gave no sign that he had ever heard Lem's voice.

'I said: was that you insulting me?' Lem stormed. 'Look at me when I'm talking to you, you yellow-bellied bastard!'

The room had gone deathly quiet and the only sound was the scrape and click of the young cowpuncher's eating irons. He was eating with serious attention to his plate, and looking nowhere else in the room. Karl felt unease stirring in his mind. What had started out as Lem's usual foul temper was heading for trouble.

'Lem!' he started, reaching out a restraining hand, but he had left it too late.

Lem was on his feet and reaching for the gun before Karl realized what he was going to do. He made a desperate grab at his brother's sleeve, but missed and the gun came out of the holster smoothly and with the speed of a striking rattler.

It came level; Karl saw the thumb pull back the

hammer and heard feet scrabbling on the floor as bystanders threw themselves out of the way.

'No, Lem!'he bawled. 'Don't shoot!'

But Lem was in the grip of one of his rages. As the gun came level he pulled the trigger.

He had intended to put a shot across in front of the eating man's face, but as he fired, the cowboy leaned forward to take a bite of impaled steak from his fork, and the shot went straight through his head.

He was dead before his head hit the table. As he fell, the fork, jammed between his teeth, was driven through his mouth and into the back of his throat. He fell as though boneless, sideways on to the floor.

There was a moment of paralysed silence in the room, then the girl screamed. The sound seemed to release everybody from their shock, and Karl realized that things had gone too far for him to retrieve the situation.

He came to his own feet, gun in hand, and his brothers did the same. Together, they dominated the room, and Karl shoved Pink towards the archway into the saloon, where shuffling feet could be heard and voices were already being raised.

'Keep 'em out of here, Pink,' he snapped. 'Don't let nobody draw a gun, or we're all dead.'

Donny was making for the girl singer, and Karl let him. A girl that pretty with a voice which everybody in the town must know and love was a hostage worth taking.

One of the men recovered his voice enough to

shout: 'What in Hades did you do that for?'

'He was going for his gun!' snapped Lem. 'We all seen him reach! You seen it, didn't you, Karl? He was reaching! He was reaching!'

'He ain't got a gun,' said one of the men. 'Ain't nobody here got a gun. It's the town rule. When a herd's passing through, nobody can carry a gun. That way, we don't get no gunplay, nobody gets shot accidental.'

Karl realized he was right. The only guns in sight were those carried by him and his brothers.

'Who made the rule?' he asked.

'Town constable. We all voted, and it works.'

This time, it didn't. This time, there was a dead man. Karl did not greatly care about the victim. If he decided to ignore what was plainly a threat, it was his own fault.

'He should have done what my brother said,' he snarled. 'Death's his own fault.'

'He couldn't hear what your brother said,' replied the spokesman. 'He was stone deaf. Got blowed up years ago when they was cutting the road through the mesa. He never heard anything and he never had a chance. Your murdering brother shot him for nothing.'

There was a growl of assent. The men in the room might be disarmed, but they were not cowed. There was a general movement to rise. Karl realized he was about to lose control of the situation. Even if they did not care what the consequences might be, he and the brothers could not shoot every man in the room.

Sooner or later somebody would pull them down.

'Stay in your seats, or the girl dies,' he growled. 'And don't think I won't do it. We got nothing to lose now. One girl ain't going to make a difference one way or t'other.'

The movement stopped. The men in the room sat where they were, but the waves of hatred coming from them were thick enough to drown a cow. Karl began to sweat as he realized the position he was in.

Sure, there were no guns in the saloon, but there would be plenty of guns in the town. Somewhere there was the local lawman, too, and he would not have hung up his gun.

He glanced at the back of the room. Sure enough, there was a landing and a gallery around the upper storey of the building, off which led the bedrooms. Every bedroom would have a window, and there were only four of them. They could not guard every window.

They needed a fort where they could keep their hostage. Hostages, he corrected himself. They needed more women, and maybe a child or two. Children in danger turned tough men into dummies.

It had been dark when they rode into town, but he had a memory of barred windows.

'You!' he pointed at the girl, sitting silent near Donny. 'Where's the jail?'

She stared at him. 'The jail? In the main street. You passed it coming in.'

'Take us there.' He reached out and grabbed her arm roughly. There was a growl of anger from the

53

room, and he put the barrel of the gun against her head.

'First man to pull any kind of trick kills little Miss Whippoorwill here! We got nothing to lose, but you have – the prettiest voice in the prettiest girl in the territory! Now, missy, you lead me to that jailhouse. And you walk right pretty too, or I'll put an ounce of lead through that fine throat of yours.'

Move fast, his mind told him. Move fast before it occurs to them that a man with a gun can shoot me right now and save her. Once we're inside that jail, they have to do what you say, but until then, you're relying on shock.

With his gun still pressed against her head, he hustled the girl through the outside bar and into the street. The customers sat tight while he was passing, but as soon as he was on the street he could hear the feet pounding on the floor. The batwing doors burst open, and Pink shot the first man through them. The crowd behind him fell back.

'The jail, missy. Right now! Move!'

The girl led them down the street to the adobe he remembered. The door of the office was open, and he pushed her through. As he did so, he heard booted feet scrape on the floor and a surprised voice said : 'Hello, Annie! What brings you here?'

Karl stepped into the room, to find a thickset man in a black leather vest standing up from behind a desk. There was a star on the front of his vest and Pink, following in, shot him through it. The peace officer did not even have a chance to reach for his gun.

The girl gave a shrill gasp and made to run to the dying man, but Karl caught her by the hair and dragged her back.

'You move when I say and not until,' he told her. 'I got nothing to lose, now.'

Thanks to fat, stupid Lem, his mind told him. When this was over, he swore to himself for the umpteenth time, he would cut free of his damned brothers and go off on his own. But for now: 'Put her in a cell and watch her,' he said. 'She's our ticket out of here.'

He turned to Donny in time to see his brother's eyes following the girl as Lem grabbed her arm, and pushed her towards the door at the back of the office. It opened on to a short corridor between two barred compartments. One of them was quite small, and had a cot against the wall, supported by two chains. The other was much bigger and had four bunks in it. At the end of the corridor was a heavy wooden door studded with iron rivets and closed with two massive bolts. It opened, when he looked out, into a corral which was empty.

'Put her in the single cell,' he said. 'We'll get some more to go in the big one. I'll go find them. The more we have, the more the town has to lose.'

With Donny to help him he let himself out of the rear door of the jail and made his way along the backs of the buildings near it, peering into lighted windows. There had to be women and kids through one of them.

CHAPTER FIVE

Obadiah Peabody watched events unfold from the loft of the livery stable, where he had spread his blankets, for once, under a roof. He was not used to sleeping under cover, and much preferred to sleep in the open where he could hear events unfolding before they had a chance to jump him.

He heard the gunshot from the saloon and correctly judged it was fired by one of the four men he had brought into town with guns on their hips. The migrants with the wagons had stayed with their livestock and womenfolk, so the only people in town who would not know about the 'no guns' rule would be the four hard men who came in with the wagons.

He knew what they were if he did not yet know who. He had seen the same combination of fine horseflesh and bad men many times in his long, hard life, and it always meant one thing: the good horses were needed because their owners expected to have to get away from something, somewhere or someone as fast as they could.

Lawmen do not go on the run, so unless these were four of the least likely rangers he had ever seen, they were bad actors, acting badly.

Usually, Obadiah handled such men methodically. He avoided trouble when he could and killed it when he could not. There were four of these men, and Obadiah was not as fast as he once had been, so he relied on his considerable guile to handle them rather than his guns.

But this time it was different. This time they had taken a hostage, and the hostage they had taken was very important to Obadiah. She was the daughter – all right, the granddaughter – he had always wanted but never had.

He had generated children, all right. He had in his life taken four wives, and buried all four of them. Two had been Indians and their children still lived with their mothers' people. He had seen them from time to time and acknowledged them according to the rites and customs of their mothers' people.

He found it ironic that the Indians – two of his offspring were Apache and three more Tohono O'Odham from the deep south west of the Territory – accepted his children, but in white men's society they would be rejected as half-caste and inferior.

'Kids is kids,' he opined. 'Didn't ask to be born, didn't choose the colour of their skins. Don't matter, nohow. They're kids and they're there.'

By his two white wives he had no offspring, though

he did not know why. One had been killed in an Indian raid on his cabin while he was away. She had not died easy and he tracked down the small raiding party which had killed her, and left their heads on stakes round their campfire.

The other died in childbirth in his arms. He buried her and the body of the tiny boy who had killed her under their cabin and burned the cabin down over the grave so that it would not be found and defiled. He was lonely after her death for the first time in his life, and when he came across Annie the singer, he was captivated by her music. After a while she came to fill the emptiness in his heart. He had been on his way to see her when he had come across Jan Paulus and his little caravan.

Because Annie had been singing when he arrived, and he knew that she would stop when she knew he was around, he had stayed in the saloon, listening, and decided to visit her the following morning, when she had rested.

Now she was a hostage, and he blamed himself for it, bitterly. He had brought the four killers to town, he had left her to their mercies when he went to rest. It logically became his responsibility to put right the wrong he had allowed to happen. He planned to kill them, naturally. But he also planned for her to survive the experience, and she had better be unhurt, or the four men he had brought would suffer for it, terribly.

He watched Karl and Lem Indianing their way along the back of the cabins, peering in at the windows and knew at once what they were doing. They were looking for more hostages, and because of the men they were, Karl and Lem would go for women and children as being easier to intimidate and eventually to kill.

It was an indication of how far these men had turned aside from the traditions of Western society that they even considered harming a respectable woman. Most Western men had an almost mystical regard for respectable white women. Their indignation if a woman was harmed usually ran to tall trees and short ropes.

But to a man who had stepped outside the conventions of Western society a woman made an ideal hostage. A woman will do what she is told to keep her child from harm and a man will behave himself to protect his womenfolk.

Obadiah slipped soundlessly across the loft and dropped out of the loading hatch at the end into the corral. The migrants' livestock moved restlessly as he slipped between them, but he smelled of the open spaces, of woodsmoke and sweat, and they were used to those smells, so they were not unduly alarmed.

Paulus and his wife were sitting by the fire, drinking coffee while the other migrants bedded down. The men and boys slept with their guns in their blankets under the wagons. It would be a foolhardy outlaw who tried to kidnap from this camp, even if there were not guards out there in the darkness, and Obadiah knew that there were, and where they were.

He slipped between them until he was close enough to Paulus to make himself known, and then spoke out of the darkness.

'Paulus? Don't look round.' The man just controlled a spasmodic leap of surprise, which made him jerk comically. He covered it by dropping his coffee cup, swearing, and bending low to pick it up again, then rising to refill it. When he sat down again, he was facing Obadiah, but looking down into his coffee mug. It covered the movement of his lips.

'Obadiah? What's up?'

'All hell to pay in the town, horse. Those four men you come in with.'

Paulus drank coffee and spat into the embers.

'What did they do?'

'There was shooting trouble back in the saloon. Then they went to the jail. More shooting there. Who, I don't know yet. Lawman, maybe. Leastwise, he ain't stopped them holing up there and they got a hostage. A girl.'

'What?' Paulus was so tense Obadiah thought he would hear him twang. 'Who?'

'Singer from the saloon. My . . . my granddaughter.' Not true, but that was genuinely the way he thought of Anne.

Some of the tension went out of Paulus, and Obadiah wondered why.

'Now they're out looking for more. All your folk snugged up safe?'

The tension was back. Paulus could not control his

feelings, and stood up suddenly.

'Betty! Betty's in town. She went in to visit her Aunt Hepsibah who lives here. That's why we took the Mormon Trail down here, to see if we can talk Hepsie into going to California with us.'

Paulus was reaching for his rifle, and Obadiah knew he could not stop him.

'Get your people awake and forted up. I don't think they'll try you frontal. But you corner a rat and he'll go for you. What we got here's four rats, and they're on the run. Where'd Betty go?'

Paulus was poking the men and women awake and his wife was pouring water on the fire. The lanterns were doused. The sleeping camp turned instead into an armed and alert camp, bristling with guns. Silence fell with the darkness. The only light came from the lanterns in the town, and any intruders would be outlined against them.

Obadiah heard movement in the darkness and waited until he could see Paulus's profile outlined against the lights of the town before he leaned forward and touched him. The man jumped, then realized who it had to be and said: 'Obadiah?'

'Naw, Abraham Lincoln. Who'd you expect out here, horse?'

'Well, Abe wouldn't ha' give me as big a shock, you old sidewinder. We better go and get Betty before she gets into trouble. It's the third cabin up and the left-hand side of the main street. Got a porch and a front gate.'

But Betty already was in trouble and so was her aunt. The front door of the house was standing open when they arrived, slipping out of the darkness like a pair of raiding Comanches. There was a plate with cake on it standing on the table, and genteel cups and saucers had been laid. One was overturned and the contents had run out and ruined a white lace table-cloth. Paulus righted it absent-mindedly, while Obadiah poked his head carefully round doorposts. The house was empty, and the only disorder was in the main room around the table.

Both Betty and her Aunt Hepsibah had gone.

Paulus swore, bitterly, once. Then he looked out of the door and up the street to where the jail stood like a block of solid stone among the wood and false-fronts. There was a light in there, and people could be seen moving around through the small, barred window.

As they watched a man stepped out of the shadows across the street from the jail. He was carrying a bundle which wriggled, and he was heading for the jail.

'Can't let him do that, horse,' said Obadiah and he was gone from Paulus's side before the wagon master could move. Out in the street, a shape flick-ered into and out of the light from the lamp outside the jail and there was a scuffle of feet and a few puffs of dust went up, caught in the lamplight, then the man carrying the package was thrown on his face and the package was gone.

Obadiah stepped on to the porch and handed a wriggling child to Paulus. It was a little girl and she was terrified. Paulus, uncertain what to do, held her close, and felt the little body stiffen in his grasp.

'It's OK, little one. We're here to help you,' he said desperately. 'Where do you live? Where's your Mom?'

A small arm pointed to the house across the street. They stepped into the shadows and circled to approach the house from behind. The back door was open and a distraught woman was staring out, panic on her face. She grabbed the child as soon as she saw it, and waved a butcher's knife as big as a machete at them.

'It's all right, Mommy! They saved me!' her daughter reassured her. The knife fell on the floor and the woman burst into tears, clasping the child to her.

Obadiah stared at her for a moment, then shrugged, closed the open door and upended the heavy kitchen table against it. Then he walked to the front door which gave on to the street, and locked that, wedging it closed with a bench.

'You got a gun in the house, ma'am?' he asked. The woman pointed at the fireplace, where a Sharps carbine hung on pegs. Paulus took it down and checked that it was loaded. It was. He handed it to her.

'Anybody you don't know tries to get in, shoot

him,' he said. 'Right smack dab through the brisket, ma'am. And don't miss, for he won't.'

'But suppose it's an innocent bystander?' she asked.

Obadiah grinned at her. 'You can always say sorry later,' he said. 'Best put your back agin' something when you fire, though. Sharps kick a bit. You got a window upstairs?'

She nodded.

'We'll go thataway, horse,' he said, and was gone like a smelly shadow. Paulus gave her a weak grin and followed him. They dropped from the window in the end gable of the house and found themselves ankle-deep in a vegetable plot. Paulus knew what labour would be needed to raise vegetables in this country, and paid silent respect.

They crept up on the back of the jail where they found four horses in the corral, and saddles racked on the corral poles. The outlaws were building a headquarters and they were making sure their escape route was allowed for, too.

Obadiah crept between the horses without disturbing them, and tried the massive rear door to the building. It was, as he expected, locked, and after a careful examination of the door by touch he knew it was too strong to open with anything but blasting powder.

That left the barred windows. He examined them and tried the strength of the bars as far as he could. They were solidly set and there was no sign of loose mortar, so he knew that they, too, would take considerable force to remove.

He caught hold of the bars and lifted himself until he could see through the windows. He found, as he had expected, that he was looking into the cells. There was a lantern burning in the little passageway and he could see the three captured women in there. There were two children with them as well, which told him the outlaws had abandoned any reservations about their behaviour. After this, every man's hand would be against them, and he hoped they were not expecting to enjoy a long and sunny old age. For them, just making it to next week was going to be an achievement.

He let himself down and scouted the surroundings of the corral.

The jail had been built in the middle of what had become the main street, and the other buildings had grown up around it. To its north and south the road stretched out into the desert, but to the east and west the town was beginning to straggle out.

Behind the corral was an open stretch of ground, bordered with huts leaning huddled against one another. Lights showed through canvas walls and from under tar-paper roofs. There was a steady hum of sounds, indistinctly heard conversations, the occasional raised voice.

Obadiah's face hardened as he looked at the scene. He detested towns with their crowded humanity, their smells and their noise. For a moment the lure of his open mountains, his forests and his deserts tugged at him, but he had a job to do and his beloved Annie needed him. He turned from the crowded huddle and walked silently round it.

To the north of the jail there was a stable with another corral behind it. Two horses stood there, nose to tail, snoozing on their feet in the night's cool air. Soon it would become truly cold; these mounts obviously knew it and stayed together for warmth.

There came a whisper of movement along the side of the jail, and Paulus was with him. The two men moved away from the corral and hunkered down to talk.

'All of them in there now,' Paulus reported. 'Town's quiet, mainly. The men are gathered in the saloon, talking about how to get their women and kids back. Not getting anywhere, for all the palaver. But sooner or later they're going to bust out. Tempers are running pretty high, and them as didn't lose their womenfolk and kids is all for breaking in and getting them out.'

'Understandable. I feel jumpy as a horned toad sitting on a cactus myself. But any man tries to bust in there's going to set a massacre going. Them owlhoots got nothing to lose, and we have.'

Paulus nodded in the gloom. 'What we need is something'll get them out in the open where we can get at 'em. But what?'

Obadiah shook his head. 'Getting them out's no problem. They gotta come out, and right soon. Can't stay in there for ever. They need water and food, and they'll start demanding things soon. Come daylight, they'll have a list, and they ain't daft enough to come out of that jail all at the one time. One at least's got to stay in to guard the women and young 'uns.'

'So what we going to do?'

'For now, we wait. They ain't thirsty, yet.'

CHAPTER SIX

But they were, and not only for water.

Inside the jail tempers were running high and fraying fast.

'So tell us again about this kid you lost,' Pink was saying. Since Lem had come staggering back from his foray to find more hostages with a lump on his head and nothing to show for his absence, the others looked at him with suspicions eyes, and Pink's suspicion could run to shooting.

'Ain't nothing to tell,' Lem snarled. The lump on the side of his head hurt abominably. He had grabbed the child and run. It was only a matter of a few hundred yards, and he had easily controlled the child's wild struggles. Then, as he was home and dry, the sky fell on his head.

He had come to in the street, his mouth full of dirt and his head full of pain. He wanted, very badly, to hurt somebody, and there were helpless people in the jail. His brothers controlled him with difficulty.

'Iffen you start on these hostages, how we going to get out of here?' Karl growled at him. 'They're our tickets out. While they're safe, them yokels out there have to do what they bin told. Hurt them and what's to stop them there citizens boiling in here and stringing us up to the nearest tree?'

There was a suitable tree just out of town on the north side. They had all seen it as they rode in, and nobody had any illusions why there was a length of frayed rope still hanging from one of the stouter branches.

Donny was less worried about the outcome. Typically, he had become obsessed with the two girls locked in the cells, and he seemed to be able to think of nothing else. Karl knew the signs and realized that he had a serious problem, whether they were in or out of the jail.

He had another problem, too. The posse from Hardwick might have dropped behind a lot, but they would still be coming right along. They might have run into Indian trouble or lost the trail or simply stopped overnight to rest their horses, but they would be coming right along, all right. He had never seen such a dogged crew.

For the hundredth time he wondered what had activated this particular lot. He had been pursued before, but not with this venomous determination. This posse seemed to have come right from the heart of hell.

Mentally, he ran over the events in Hardwick once

again. The hold-up, the spatter of shooting, the accidental wounding of the pretty girl, and the resulting relentless chase.

He could see nothing in these events which should have made this such a nightmare. The wounding of the girl was unfortunate, all right, but it had been purely accidental, and the people in the bank must know that. In his mind there was always some excuse for his own actions, and one of them was regularly that he didn't mean anybody any harm and they would have been perfectly all right if they just got out of his way.

There was a scuffle and a muffled cry from the cells, and he was on his feet and in the corridor between the cages, gun in hand and fury in his heart within a second. Donny, his face marked with a row of parallel scratches, was just backing out of the end cell, and the pretty Betty O'Donnell, her hair awry, was crouching with her hands curled into claws in the middle of the little cell. The front of her dress had been torn, and she was panting desperately.

'You put a hand to me again, you . . . you owlhoot, and I'll blind you!' she hissed. Behind her in the cell the woman who said she was the girl's aunt, was in an almost identical position, though he noticed her clothes had not been interfered with.

He grabbed his brother by his hair and pulled him out of the cell corridor. When the door fell shut, he took a long swing and smacked the Colt across the bridge of his nose. He felt the bone break. Donny

70

screamed like a woman and almost fell to his knees. Blood poured from his nose.

'You broke my nose!' he sobbed. 'You broke my nose!' Comically it came out as : 'You broke by dose,' and Lem cackled.

'Go past that door one more time, you bastard, and I'll break your goddam neck!' Karl told him. 'We got to get the hell out of here, and we got to get out soon. Them women and kids're all we got between us and a rope, and you want to throw that away! Keep your jeans buttoned and your hands in your pockets or I swear I'll kill you!'

He grabbed Donny's collar and dragged him up until the two men were only inches apart.

'I swear I will kill you. You got that? I'll goddam bury you, right here, in Hicksville, Noplace, Nowhere Territory and the goddam dust won't even bother to gather on your sorry grave! You got that?'

Eyes smouldering with hatred glared back at him. He could hear Donny's breath bubbling in the ruin of what had been a fine-drawn nose, and realized that he had by chance hurt his brother in the one way he would neither forgive nor forget. His looks.

He was too angry at this moment to draw the obvious conclusion from this, but as the night wore on he came to understand that he would never again be able to turn his back on Donny without risk.

He would live to regret it, but at this moment he was more worried about the dangers without than those within his family.

Pinks's and Lem's eyes were on him as he turned away, and he could not read what they meant.

He pulled the top off the water *olla* hanging in the corner and tipped it to run a stream over his head. It was not cold inside the jail, and the water was warm and brackish but it was at least wet. He filled his hand and wiped down his face at the same time.

Pink watched the performance with stony eyes. Neither he nor Lem made any attempt to intervene or help Donny wash his face.

'Somebody make some coffee,' snapped Karl. 'It's gonna be a long night!'

Outside in the street it was turning into a desperate night, too. The meeting in the saloon had broken up and there were men in doorways all down the row of buildings.

But not one of them was carrying a firearm. Crouching there in the dark, they wielded weapons ranging from old cavalry sabres and Bowie knives to billhooks and mallets, and one Indian lance somebody's father reckoned he had found at the Little Big Horn. They were desperate men and desperate men will take up what is to hand.

A number collected in the alleyway across the street from the jail. The dark was hardly disturbed by the lanterns in the street, but Obadiah could see almost as well as a cat in the dark, and he could see no firearms.

'Where's the guns?' he asked, puzzled.

'In the jail,' said the bartender from the saloon, who was picked out in the gloom by his white apron. Paulus growled at him to take it off, and after a moment, he did.

'What, all of them, horse? All in the jailhouse? Why, in the name o' Cochise and all the Indians? What good are they there?'

He was told that their late sheriff had collected all the handguns and rifles in town and locked them away in the jailhouse, where, unknown to the bandits, they lay at this moment.

'You mean, there ain't no weepons in town? Nary a single one?' Obadiah was incredulous.

'They're in town, all right. They just ain't in our hands,' he was told. His informant was quite impressed by the venom and fluency of the language which exploded from the old Indian fighter's lips.

The little knot of men split roughly into two camps: the ones who thought a frontal attack on the jail was the only answer, and the ones who for one reason or another, cared most deeply about the fate of the hostages.

The one thing they had in common was that neither set had any firearms. The rule laid down by the sheriff was that no firearms were to be kept while the trail herds were passing through, either by the residents or the herders. All had been gathered in and locked into a stone cellar below the jail, the entrance to which was a trapdoor behind the sheriff's desk. On it was the sheriff's chair and in the chair was, generally, the sheriff.

Karl was currently sitting on that chair which meant he was sitting on the town's arsenal.

Obadiah and Jan Paulus stared at one another. The light from the nearest lantern was faint, but neither had any difficulty reading his opposite number's thoughts. They were, give or take a good strong cuss word or so, identical.

An unarmed town in the Painted Desert, surrounded by Indians and on the main route north and south for immigrants, travellers good and bad, and trail herds was a sitting target for any passing outlaw, and four of those passing outlaws had just stopped off.

'You mean, you ain't got no guns a-tall?' Obadiah had to be certain he had not misunderstood.

'None,' said the bartender from the saloon.

'Now why, in the name of all that's holy, did the sheriff disarm the town?'

Feet shuffled. Eventually one man said: 'Can't ask the trail herders to hock their guns if the townsfolk keep theirs. Stands to reason. Works, too. We ain't had no trail herd killings in three years. And we get the guns back when the herd's gone on through.'

Obadiah spat a stream of tobacco juice into the dust. It hit with considerable force.

'So there ain't no guns a-tall in town except in that there hoosegow?'

There was a slight disturbance at the back of the group, and a voice said: 'Well, actually, *señor*, yes there are.'

There was a shuffling in the group and a young man stepped through. There was a murmur from the assembled citizens, which was not altogether friendly, and in the dim light, Paulus shot a look at Obadiah.

'You say you got guns?'

'I sell guns, *señor*. I am the gunsmith here.'

Paulus stared round at the shadowy group of men gathered in the half-light. With the only light coming from above, their faces were in shadow, but there was a definite atmosphere of hostility and shuffled feet.

'How many guns you got?'

'Not enough to arm the town, but enough to make a difference, *señor*. Also shells. I have shells.'

Paulus said: 'Go and get them. Bring them here.'

The young man leaned forward and for the first time his face came into the light. He was strikingly good-looking, with a dark face with high cheekbones and a mane of hair which looked black in the gloom. It had been caught with a length of thong to hang down his back. The lantern caught the dull gleam of an earring in one lobe, and his shirt was closed at the neck with a length of leather run through a big, elaborate, silver medallion.

'I will need help, *señor*. They are many.'

'Rifles or hand guns?'

'But both, *claramente*. They are my stock in trade.'

There was an edge to the comment, and Obadiah caught it and wondered.

'You'll get them back, horse. Soon as we've made

good use of them. The town'll pay you for the shells. What's the name? I ain't come across you afore.'

'I am Tomas Delgado, *señor*. I arrive here only recently, to set up my business.'

They shook hands, and two men volunteered to go with Delgado to collect the weapons. The others, beyond shuffling uncomfortably, did not comment, though Obadiah noticed a few glances being exchanged.

The arming party reappeared soon enough, carrying a collection of rifles and a bucket of handguns.

Delgado was humping a box of cartridges, and Obadiah, who had a shrewd idea of how much a box of shells would weigh, noticed he carried them on one crooked arm without apparent effort. This, he realized, was a man strong beyond his appearance.

'I brought .44s, *señor*,' Delgado explained as he levered the top off the crate and stripped back the foil which kept the ammunition dry.

'Why?' growled the bartender, who was part of the group which was not happy in the gunsmith's company.

'Because it fits both the Winchesters and the .44 Colts,' said Delgado simply. 'We do not need range. This will be a firefight in the main street, once they are out of the jail. The pistols lose range because they have shorter barrels. The rifles can use the same shells, but shoot them further. The charge is confined within the longer barrel for longer, and has greater force. Also . . .'

He sounded like a man who, once he had warmed to his subject, might never leave it, and something was happening over at the jail.

'We'll talk about it later,' said Paulus, hastily. He was handing out the guns to the nearest of the men who were crowding into the little alleyway. In all, the young gunsmith had managed to arm a dozen. It was a strong start.

'Spread out along the street, where you can see the jail entrance,' Obadiah issued instructions. 'You two – what's your names, horse? OK, Jed and Lucas, you come with me round the back.'

He led them along the backs of the cabins facing the street until they could cross unseen from the building, then he crossed over and set them up behind the jail, with a clear shot at the rear door.

'They got their hostages, so you don't fire unless you got a clear field o' fire, OK, horse? I don't want a drop of them women's blood spilled. You take particular care you don't go shooting nowhere near my Annie. Not nowhere near her, horse, or you are going to miss out on a whole lot of that lovely singing of hers. Clear?'

One of the men said dubiously: 'How come?'

'On account of I'll hang your head on the bar, horse, right where she could be heard best – but you won't be listening, horse, on account of your body will be in Boot Hill Do I make myself clear, horse?

Real, crystal clear?'

'Like a bright May morning,' said the questioner, fervently. Even in the dark he could have sworn he could see the glitter of the old man's eyes, and neither he nor his friend doubted for a split second that the old Indian fighter meant what he said. The town knew Obadiah of old, and knew he was a stringy old man who smelled of leather and sweat and whiskey when he was in town, but he could be hell on wheels when he had his dander up.

'And his dander was up real high that night,' the man reported later. The listening townsfolk nodded sagely and devoted themselves to their drinks.

Obadiah returned on a different route to the far side of the street, where the armed men had settled themselves into comfortable positions, and were now beginning to feel the cold and the tension in the waiting.

As he settled himself and found a place to rest his long barrel, the door of the jail was eased open, and a lantern was swung out to stand on the boardwalk.

'Hey! You out there!' called Lem, without showing himself outside the darkened doorway.

'What you want?' called one of the townsfolk before Obadiah could stop him.

'We need water, and food and a bottle of whiskey,' Lem bellowed. 'Bring them to the front of the jail, now!'

This time Obadiah got his word in before the self-appointed spokesman.

'No deal!' he roared. 'What you willing to trade for 'em?'

'Trade? We ain't trading! You do what you're told, and quick. We got your hostages.'

'Oh, yeah? Says who? How do we know what you got in there? Show us what you got, horse – and be mighty quick about it, or we start shooting!'

He could hear the murmur of unrest all the way down the street, but the most noticeable reaction was from the jail, where there was a piercing scream, and the tousled figure of Betty O'Donnell appeared in the doorway, struggling madly.

It was a bad mistake on the part of the bandits. From up and down the street came a moan of general outrage, like the grumble of a storm in the distance. Several men started forward from their hiding-places, and stopped only when Betty was dragged back into the jail and a warning shot spat dust into the lamplight.

'Get back!' bellowed Karl. He appeared in the doorway, gun in hand, and fired down the street apparently at random. 'You come any closer and the girl dies!'

Obadiah stepped out into the lamplight, his long rifle over his arm like a man going duck shooting. He looked a ragged and bony figure, and his face was shadowed by the broad-brimmed hat.

'You want to palaver, you come out here in the open, horse. You stand face to face with me and tell me what you willing to trade for this water you ain't got in there.'

He heard quite distinctly the double click of a rifle being cocked within the jail, and raised his hand theatrically above his head.

'You start the shooting and you see where it ends, horse. They tell me the view from Boot Hill ain't all that good here. I may be there, but I'll have plenty of company with me, and you'll be in there, too.'

There was a silence, then Karl stepped out into the lamplight. He had his Colt in his hand, and he looked cautiously around into the shadows.

Obadiah laughed mockingly. 'What you expecting to see, horse? There's a hundred guns in a hundred hands out there, and every single one of them is pointing right at you. There's many men here as fought in the War Between the States. Some of them was snipers, and they never miss, so your chance of getting back in that jail depends entirely on what you say to me and I say to you.

'Best speak softly, horse, or it'll be the last thing you ever say.'

He grounded his rifle, crossed his arms and leaned on the muzzle. To the observers, he was insolently relaxed. But under the buckled brim of his hat his eyes were alert and wandering over the front of the jail. There was a face within the window, its owner standing well back and probably under the impression that he could not be seen, but Obadiah knew he could himself have dropped the man with one shot.

But where were the others? To make sure the

hostages were safe, he had to be certain all four bandits died at once, and since he could see only two, that was out of the question.

Karl was baffled by the old man's confidence. In his book, holding hostages meant holding the winning hand. The townsfolk had to do what they were told or their hostages would suffer and that was that.

'I want water and food, and I want it now,' he said. But the very fact that he had to repeat it made him sound weak, and he knew it.

Obadiah smiled slowly. 'I know what you want, horse. What I ain't heard yet is what you going to trade for it,' he said.

'Trade? I ain't trading, I'm telling you! Water, food, and whiskey. And that damn fast! Or them ladies in there going to find us real friendly. Real friendly and passionate. You get my drift?'

He thrust his chin forward aggressively and realized his mistake too late. The muzzle of the long rifle was suddenly under his jaw and Obadiah jerked it upwards with cruel accuracy. It smashed into Karl's jaw, slamming his teeth together. They caught the tip of his tongue, and he felt, through a mist of pain, the hot blood run down his chin.

'I ask you a civil question, and you talk dirty to me, you polecat dropping? You want something from me and this town, you goddam better have something to trade that this town wants. You get your water when we get one of them women back. Two of them, and you get food. All of them and you get to leave town.'

He leaned forward and stared into Karl's eyes. 'There's one of your brothers watching this through that window, and he ain't done a mortal thing to stop me breaking your face, which is exactly what I thought he'd do. You expect to get backed up, you gonna need some guys better than you got. Now, I'll say it again: turn one of them gals loose, and she better be unhurt. You know for why? I had two Indian wives in my time, and I lived with their folks a while. Still got young 'uns with them.

'They got some right nasty tricks with a skinning knife, them Apaches. Can keep a prisoner alive for days. Make you weep to hear them guys scream.

'You don't want to find out how, you better start thinking straight, horse. One girl out, water in. Two girls out, food. All of 'em, you get to ride out of here.'

Even in the gloom, Karl could see the old man's eyes glittering. The words in the low voice fell on the street like slabs of lead.

'Choice is yours, horse. Don't make me come for you at dawn. By dawn, I'll be good and mad. You wouldn't like me when I'm mad, and it'd take us days to get the blood offen that white wall.'

Suddenly, Karl was standing alone in the middle of the darkened street, with blood dripping from his chin. He swallowed and winced. His tongue began to really hurt.

He felt like a fool and, like his brother, he wanted

to hurt somebody. But the drawling voice of the old man rustled in his memory, and he realized that he had believed, deep within his soul, every word Obadiah had uttered.

Their stronghold had turned back into a prison, and they had put themselves there.

How to get out? How, in the name of all that was holy, were they going to get out?

CHAPTER SEVEN

Tomas Delgado knew he was not universally liked in Painted Rock. For one thing, he had been identified as a Mexican, which was half true. He was the product of a marriage between a Spanish officer and an Apache woman.

Their union had delighted neither of their peoples. She defied her people to marry the dark, handsome man in the uniform of the Mexican army. He identified himself as a 'squaw man' and was rejected by the officer class to which he had been born.

It broke neither of their hearts, and when he settled north of what was to become the border, he was, surprisingly, accepted by her Mescalero Apache people. They treated him at first with suspicion, then with a guarded caution, and eventually when he fought as fiercely as they against the various bands of scalp hunters and intruders to their lands, he was accepted as a warrior. It helped that he was a clever man, a fine shot and a tracker almost up to the exacting standards of his adopted people.

Like them, he was a warrior and a brave one.

Tomas as a child grew up in the Apache tradition. He went through the Indians' initiation to manhood and, because he was not exactly as his contemporaries were, he tried harder and he achieved at least what they did, though he was astute enough to avoid outstripping them, though he might with effort have done so.

He found that because of his father's expertise with guns he also had a grasp of how they worked and why. At first grudgingly and later eagerly, his Apache companions brought their problems to him to solve, and he learned how to do a remarkably good job with the materials and tools at hand.

His father watched his progress, and did his best to encourage the boy, finding him tools and at first helping him, then later watching with pride the expertise he was acquiring. In the end he spent some of his small store of money sending his son to a school set up by the Jesuit priests in one of the presidios established by the Spanish when they colonized the south west.

It was not entirely a blessing. He found the preaching and tight restrictions of the fathers' faith hard to accept, since he had been brought up in the Apache traditions. The Indians' relationship with the desert and its inhabitants seemed to him to be far closer to what he knew of the mysteries of nature and of tribal life. The mysticism of both faiths was hard for him to accept, but he could see more sense in the Indians' relationships with their land than in the mysticism of the Jesuits.

After the first couple of beatings, which were savage because of the outrage his outspoken opinions provoked, he learned to keep his mouth shut and his scepticism behind his teeth, and he and his mentors rubbed along well enough.

But the blood which ran in his veins was as much his mother's as his father's, and when he was presented with a dilemma he opted for his mother's traditions, beat the daylights out of the boy who had been trying to bully him into submission, stole food and a water bottle, and took a carbine and a bag of ammunition from the guardhouse.

Cannily, he did not steal a horse, because that would have meant for certain a ruthless pursuit and probably a bullet when they caught him. He took to the desert behind the presidio, and loped in a long loop through the night, concealing his tracks where it was possible and confusing them where it was not.

He sat in a nest of rocks miles from the fortified chapel, and watched the cloud of dust that he knew indicated his pursuers set off in the wrong direction. Then he continued his journey and arrived back home a few days later.

His parents received him with mixed feelings. His mother was joyful, her husband more cautious, though he relaxed considerably when he was assured that young Tomas had left no bodies behind him, and stolen no horses.

There was no further pursuit, and among his contemporaries the theft of the carbine and ammunition brought him much admiration, and not a little envy.

The carbine was his first professional job. Badly looked after and short barrelled, it was wildly inaccurate, and he settled down to find out why. He took the weapon down to its constituent parts, found what was wrong with it – mostly because of unenthusiastic maintenance – and put the faults right. When he had finished it was a different weapon. Its breechblock worked smoothly and reliably, its trigger action was as crisp as lettuce, its sights painstakingly accurate. He made his own ammunition and improved its range, though there was little he could do about the length of its stubby barrel, or its savage recoil.

By the time he had finished it other warriors were keen for him to work on theirs as well, and he invariably improved the weapons, often with the smallest amount of attention.

He was a gunsmith.

It was not long before he realized that if he could fix the Indian guns, which were often antiques and almost invariably in poor condition, he could fix anything else. It also occurred to him that if he wanted a steady supply of parts and new weapons, he needed to make the money to buy them.

Apaches did not have money unless they stole it

from white men, so he went to the source of supply. Within a few years he had built up a good business in one of the little towns down near the San Carlos reservation, but the repeated rumbles of unrest among the Apaches corralled up there by the government made white men steer clear of the area, and they took their business with them.

He took his stock and his money, put them on pack mules, and headed north. Painted Rock was the first town he found which did not have a gunsmith, and he rented a cabin as close to the centre of town as he could, set up a shooting range behind it with a solid rock backstop, and went into business.

He was not popular among a certain element of the town's rougher men, who distrusted him as a half-breed, but his honesty and his expert work gradually established him as a trusted and eventually even a valued citizen.

He was also a remarkable shot, and tonight, comfortably settled behind the wooden parapet of the saloon roof, where he could see the front of the jail and even had a restricted view of the corral behind it, he cuddled the stock of his rifle to his cheek. He was mildly amused by the ease with which Obadiah had reversed the situation, and made the bandits prisoners instead of jailers. But he was far more worried about the fact that Anne Prescott was one of the hostages in the jailhouse.

He had been in love with Annie since he had first seen her, but had never had the courage to approach her. Now, he was agonized at the thought that she was a prisoner, and did not know that he loved her. Once she was out, he promised himself, he would tell her, and take the consequences.

Tomas watched the jail carefully. He knew about the rear entrance, of course, and he knew Obadiah and of his secret adoration of Annie. At first he thought the old man ludicrously in love with her, but soon realized that Obadiah looked upon her as a granddaughter, and nothing else.

He also understood the old man's passion for his long rifle, the more so when he realized that Obadiah had actually made the weapon himself, and even cut its rifling lands. He had seen Obadiah doing target practice one morning, and, a good shot himself, was awed by the old man's uncanny accuracy. He had heard of the technique of the 'wandering aim' but never seen it practised before.

What it amounted to was allowing the long barrel to wander around and fire when it passed over the target. Obadiah did not miss once. When he had finished, he cocked an eye over his shoulder to where Tomas thought he had been standing unobserved, and called: 'Reckon you can do better, horse?'

Tomas did not, but he could not for shame refuse the challenge, and he shot well. Eventually, Obadiah handed him the long rifle and a handful of shells and said: 'See how you can get on with her.'

The weapon was a revelation to Tomas. Despite its

great length, it was remarkably well-balanced and, even to him, it felt 'right' in his hand. Unused to the floating aim technique, he missed with the first two shots, but from then on his bullets flew true, and he handed the long rifle back reluctantly.

'I would very much like to own such a rifle,' he said. 'If you will allow me to take some measurements, I will try to make one for myself.'

He did, and it was that long-barrelled rifle which rested on the saloon parapet at this moment. Also on the roof with him was a long-barrelled Colt .44 which he had also taken to pieces and reassembled with love and expertise.

All he needed now was a target and a reassurance that his unwitting love was safe.

Inside the jail the brothers had separated into two camps. One, Karl and Pink, was for doing a deal with the old frontiersman and the townsfolk, and making a run for the towns to the south. It meant going through Apache country, but, as Karl pointed out, they were surrounded by Indians and chased by the posse. After the killing of the deaf cowpuncher they had no chance of survival if they stayed here. Even if they made threats of abuse to the hostages, they still had to get out of the jailhouse, and they would have added another posse to their trail.

Lem and Donny were all in favour of getting out, but they did not trust the word of the old woodsman. They wanted to take the women with them.

'Won't dare follow us close,' said Lem. 'Iffen they do we can always string up the old woman to a cactus. Time they get her free, get the spikes out and get her back here, we'll be long gone.'

Donny spoke less but Karl knew what was in his mind and it did not involve cactus plants. He wanted the women with him and he wanted darkness and a hiding-place.

For the thousandth time Karl wondered what he had done to deserve such brothers. Lem the vicious coward, Pink the killer, with no more emotion than a rattlesnake, and Donny the lecher. Karl had heard the word when a passing hellfire preacher had stopped off in their hometown and made the night terrible with his preaching. Karl had been a boy at the time and he did not truly know what it meant. It just sounded dreadful.

When he eventually did find out what it meant he had been amused by his own boyish dread, but when he looked at Donny it took on a new meaning, and a new hatefulness.

'We got to get out and we got to get out before morning,' he interrupted. 'Once they can see the street in daylight, they'll know which way we're heading. What's the time?'

They all looked at the old clock above the late sheriff's desk. It stood at three in the morning.

'What time's sunup?' asked Donny.

'Half after five, this time of year,' decided Karl, and saw Donny give a quick glance at the lock-up door. Two and a half hours was time aplenty for what had obviously become his obsession. Karl seriously considered killing his brother right there and then, but if they had to shoot their way out – and it looked like they would have no choice – he needed every gun and every man.

'By then we need to be clear away,' he said loudly. 'What we need is time, time out there.'

From the expressions on his brothers' faces, the idea had no appeal. They had seen the kind of shooting the old man did with that long rifle, and they did not want to experience it themselves on the receiving end. Inside the jailhouse they were behind stone walls. Outside, they were just four targets.

'Lem,' Karl said. 'Check out the back. They likely got men out there, and I want to know how many and where. If I judged that old polecat right, he'll be out front with that lodgepole of his covering the door. See who's out back.'

Lem didn't move. The idea of opening a fine solid wood door and standing out in the night air covered in just his shirt and pants clearly did not appeal to him. He sat where he was, staring back at Karl.

'Lem, you hear what I just said?'

'Sure. You just said open the door and commit suicide,' said Lem sourly. 'You want to draw some fire, you fly right at it, brother. Me, I'll wait here and count the shots.'

Karl looked round the room. All the brothers looked back at him with the same expression. Not one of them looked even inclined to step out of that door, and Pinkerton in particular had a calculating look in his eye which suggested that trying to insist might easily turn out to be fatal.

With a curse, Karl crossed the room, flung open the door to the cells, and opened the nearest one. Annie the singer looked back at him with wary eyes, and he gestured at her.

'Come here, girl. I ain't goin' to hurt you. I just need somebody to take a message out to those men out there. Tell them we'll turn you all loose so long as they give us free road out of town.'

Her expression did not change, but she stood up.

He stared at her. 'What's the matter? Don't you trust me? I'm giving you a chance to get out of here, girl. Don't you trust me?'

'How much do you weigh?' she said. He stared at her.

'Weigh? What's that got to do with it?'

'I'm trying to work out how far I could throw you. That's how far I trust you,' she said. Hot anger flared in his gut, and his gun was in his hand before he was aware of drawing it.

Her eyes closed down to slits and he found himself flinching back just at the hatred in them. Instinctively, he swung at her. The hand, heavy with the gun, caught her across the cheekbone and laid open the skin as though it had been slashed with a knife. She slapped her hand to the wound, but she did not cry out, though the blood seeped through her fingers.

He grabbed her by the hair and hauled her out into the cell corridor, ignoring the horrified cries of the other women, who had watched the whole scene unfold.

'You git out this door, and tell me what you see!' he hissed at her. 'Try and trick me, and I'll kill you myself. Now, git!'

He hauled open the door and pushed her out into the night. There was no shooting, even when he cautiously peered round the doorpost. The girl had walked to the corral, and was bending to wriggle between the rails.

'Come back here!' he hissed, but she ignored him and disappeared into the darkness. The horses moved restively in the corral, but it was too dark for him to work out where she was, anyway. After a moment, he realized that he must be outlined against the lighted cell corridor behind him, and ducked back into the jail.

No gun fired, and no lead ploughed into the doorpost. Outside was silence.

He ran back into the jailhouse and hauled Lem to his feet.

'Get up! We're going out of here, now!' he snapped.

Pink stared at him. 'How?'

'Get them hostages out of the cells and bring them through here. We send them out first and run out under cover of the women. That old turkey buzzard might talk big, but they ain't his women. The town

94

won't shoot down its own womenfolk.'

'How about horses?' Typical of Lem that his first thought should be of the means of flight.

'Ours are still at the hitching rail outside the saloon. It's not forty yards away, and if we move fast in this dark they can't be sure of hitting anything at all! But we got to move now – it's going to be light in half an hour.'

They were beginning to move even as he spoke. He opened the door to the cells, unlocked the one where Betty and her Aunt Hepsibah were and dragged them into the room.

'Lem! You take old auntie here, and Donny, you get to hide behind pretty Betty. Pink, you're with me – now, move!'

He jerked open the door, fired two quick shots at the buildings opposite, and pushed his brothers out of the door. Firing their guns, and driving the women before them, they moved out into the street. Return fire started and then abruptly stopped.

Assuming the men out there had just realized that two of the four who had come out of the jail were women, Karl grabbed Pink's sleeve.

'Come on, we go this way!' he hissed, and led the way down the corridor between the cells.

The rear door opened smoothly, and they went out without provoking any shooting. Karl swung along the back of the block and dived down an alley which led on to the main street. It brought them out opposite the saloon. Across the street, in the light from the oil lamps on the front of the saloon, their horses were tugging nervously at their halters.

Down the street, where the fugitives had come from the jail, there was a bunch of figures milling around. A woman was screaming, men were shouting, and one man – Karl thought he recognized Lem's harsh croak – was blaspheming.

Pink was in front of him when they reached the hitching rail, and as yet nobody seemed to have noticed them.

Karl grabbed the reins of his horse and was surprised to see his brother jerking the reins loose on the other two, beside his own.

'Here, you take one and I take one,' Pink snarled. He was trying to shout without raising his voice, and the result was a strangled rasp. 'Two mounts each, and we can outrun them, easy!'

Together, they abandoned their brothers to their fate and dug in their spurs. The first shots did not ring out until they were actually over the town boundary, and they came nowhere near.

They were away and free with a good start and two rested horses each.

Nothing could stop them now.

CHAPTER EIGHT

Out in the street the townsfolk were crowding round Lem and Donny, both of whom had been wounded in the outburst of firing. Aunt Hepsibah was sitting on the ground next to them, holding her right arm tightly with her left hand, while Betty, whose dress was torn but who was physically unhurt, tore strips off her petticoat to make bandages. Skin showed while she was doing it.

'Funny, that,' Obadiah, leaning on his long rifle, sounded genuinely interested. 'I been in a hundred fights. Fit Indians half my life, fit Yankees in the War Between the States, fit Quantrill and Bloody Bill Anderson after. Never seen a woman tear up her unmentionables to make bandages in real life. Nary a once.'

'Nor me neither,' agreed one of the bystanders, whose eyes were glued to Betty's bending form.

Obadiah glanced at him, then stared.

'Ain't you Lucas?' he snapped. 'What you doing

out in the street? I sent you round the back to guard the corral!'

Lucas shrugged. 'They was coming out the front, wasn't they? Knowed it all along. All the shooting was out here, so me and Jed come round to join in. Nothing happening out back.'

Tomas Delgado elbowed his way through the crowd. He looked enraged.

'They got away!' he snapped. 'While we were shooting at these two out front, the other two went out the back and got to their horses while our backs was turned. They're out on the south road, now. I saw them go, but I missed them.'

He was staring around the circle of lights, peering at faces.

'Where's Annie?' he said to the women. 'She was in there with you. She no come out at the same time?'

Betty looked up from her bandaging. 'No, they took her out the back first, and she didn't come back. Just the oldest one, Karl. He came back real mad and sent all of us out the front. I haven't seen her.'

Paulus was bending over her, holding the lantern for her. He glanced up. 'Better check the jail,' he said. Obadiah and Tomas went off at the run for the open door of the building.

Inside there was blood-spatter on the wall behind the desk, and the body of the sheriff lay face down across the trapdoor which hid the cache of guns he had confiscated. There was a boot-print on the back of his vest where one of the outlaws had stepped while reaching for the desk drawers, all of which had been pulled out and emptied on the floor. There was an open cashbox on the desk itself, and an empty cartridge box lying next to it.

'Check the back,' Tomas said. He almost got jammed in the door with Obadiah, following his own suggestion. The cells were empty, the barred doors standing open, and the rear door was pushed back against them. Outside, the first flush of morning was warming the eastern sky. The unsaddled horses were standing tranquil in the corral.

There was no sign of Annie, though both men scoured the ground for sign, and Tomas gave a grunt of surprise.

'She come this way,' he said, pointing at the scuff marks under the fence rail. Inside the corral itself the horses had milled around, and messed up whatever sign the girl had left, but the two men picked up her sign at the other side. She had, once again, slipped under the fence rail and then run for the alleyway beyond.

Together, unconsciously backing one another up, they followed her sign to the main street, where Tomas stopped short with an exclamation. The growing morning light revealed a bloody handprint on the wooden wall.

It was a slim hand, with long fingers. Tomas stared at it, his face stony.

'They have hurt her,' he said, and Obadiah muttered a curse. They ran through into the main street, where the wounded outlaws were being roughly bandaged – from their language, very roughly – and the women were being led away to Aunt Hepsibah's home. Jan Paulus's jacket was draped round his daughter's bare shoulders, though it failed to meet at the front and she seemed to be showing rather more skin than was absolutely necessary.

'No, Pa,' she was saying as he led the way, 'nobody hurt me. They was just a bit rough with me when I tried to get away.'

From Paulus's expression, being 'a bit rough' with his daughter ranked slightly above murder in the list of hanging offences. His rifle was sloping over his shoulder, but the weapon which caught Obadiah's eye in the dawn was a foot-long Bowie knife on his hip. It was the size of a bayonet and two inches across the blade. The bone handle looked well-worn.

The women were obviously safe with Paulus in town, and Obadiah told the wagon master about the fleeing bandits and the fact that they seemed to have taken Annie Preston with them.

'Why?' was Paulus's reply. Obadiah, who had his own dark suspicions, admitted he did not know for certain that she was actually with them: merely that she was gone from the jail and, judging from her tracks, had escaped across the corral. How she came to be back in the hands of the fleeing outlaws he did not know, though he had a sickening suspicion.

'I'll come with you. Let me get my horse,' Paulus said. Obadiah was about to argue when he saw the look in the wagon master's eye, and shut his mouth again. Together, he and Tomas got their own mounts from the livery stable saddled up, then they turned their horses' heads towards the trail. Paulus rode up as they hit the edge of town, and they set off at a distance-eating lope in the tracks of the fleeing outlaws.

Tomas followed the tracks carefully, with Obadiah riding off to one side and Paulus to the other in case one of the retreating men dropped off the trail. They had been moving for a while when Tomas pulled up, dismounted and hunkered down next to the tracks.

'What's up?' Obadiah asked him. He stayed at a safe distance so that he did not obscure the tracks. Paulus stayed where he was, watching the trail ahead carefully.

'Five horses. Fifth one overlays the first four in places. I don't think they are riding together,' Tomas told him. He leaned down and squinted along the line of the trail.

The new tracks were easy enough to pick out. It had been some time since anybody had ridden south along the road. The trail herds were being held east of town and were well out of the way. Nobody had left town except themselves since the outlaws had made a break for it.

'Here. And see, here to the side. The third horse

is following the first four. Tracking them at times, slowing at others – see the difference in stride? Third man hangs back where there is a chance he may be seen.

'Also, he is lighter than they. Here the print is not as deep. And here.'

Obadiah had already decided what the tracks meant.

'Not he, she. Third man is not a man, but a woman. Annie is kinda slim and light. She ain't as heavy as the men. The horse steps lighter.'

Tomas shot him a sceptical look. 'You can tell this? You, a white man?'

But he looked again at the tracks, then walked back a few paces and squatted. The road was dusty and the tracks were not sharp and clear as they would have been in mud. He straightened up.

'I cannot see the difference,' he said.

Obadiah shook his head. 'Me neither, horse,' he said. 'But where else would she be? Them owlhoots is on horses and there ain't a third with them, so they ain't grabbed her. She's been riding behind them.

'She's a proud woman, is Annie, and a handsome one. If they knew about her, they'd keep her all right. But she's also a tough one. She plays that there guitar in a saloon and no man bothers her. Take my word, horse. *No* man!'

He glanced down at the tracks.

'A proud, handsome woman. And they made her bleed. We better catch them guys up before she does, horse, or there won't be nothing left.'

Tomas shot him an incredulous look, and snorted. 'You want to save them from her? You are loco, *hombre*, loco!'

The old man looked back at him through slitted eyes that had all the compassion of a rattlesnake.

'Save them? They made my girl bleed, horse. I want to make them wish they never was born, and then I want to kill them myself with my own hands.'

There was that about his voice which made Jan Paulus's stomach muscles contract. Tomas swung back into his saddle.

'You sure you ain't at least part Apache?' he said as they moved forward. The old man did not reply, but his face said a whole bunch of things, none of them pleasant.

Together, three vengeful men rode after their enemies and the girl two of them loved.

Ahead of them, Annie was concentrating on her tracking. Her face was very painful. The savage blow from the gun had laid open her cheek, and the swelling was pulling the lips of the wound apart, no matter what she did to keep it closed. She had torn a strip off her petticoat to bind it as tightly as she could and the tightness of the bandage was at least containing the blood from the wound.

She wept for her spoiled looks. But she knew that if she was careful and left him enough sign, Obadiah Peabody would find her and his knowledge of desert plants would help. In the meantime she needed to know what the fugitives were doing and where they planned on stopping.

Annie knew they must stop soon. They had left the town without any time to prepare anything for the trail, so they would need water. More so, because she knew they had been short of water before they left.

She pulled up again, and wound the reins round her arm before dropping from the saddle. She needed to inspect the tracks the outlaws had left, and the trail was crossing a patch of hard and stony ground.

There were rules to tracking, and the first one was not to get too close to her quarry. If they even suspected that she was following them they would stop and ambush her and she had no illusions about her fate if they were successful. Whatever happened first, she would end up dead, and she had no intention of doing that.

Obadiah had talked to her long and often about looking after herself in the wild country, and she had listened more from politeness and because she liked the old man than from interest. Now, though, his words came back to her.

She distrusted any place on the trail where rocks came down too close to the road. They would be convenient for an ambush. Moving fast in the desert raised dust, so she kept her pace down to a walk. The horse had been fresh when she took it from the corral, so she did not need to worry about it becoming exhausted, at least not yet. The saddle she had borrowed from the corral rails. It belonged to the dead sheriff, so she did not need to worry about a vengeful owner on her trail. She had filled a canteen from the stable pump, so she did not need to stop for water.

Her only lack was a firearm. She had not had a chance to take one from the sheriff's cache in the jail and the 'no guns' rule meant there was none around elsewhere to take.

On the other hand, she did have a knife. It was sheathed and hung on her waist, with only the pommel showing above the band. She had taken that, too, from the stable when she got the bridle.

The sun would be hot when the day wore on, so when she tore up her petticoat as bandages she also made herself a headscarf from the rest of it, wrapping the trailing skirt round her neck. Unintentionally she had contrived a burnoose, and with several thicknesses of material it protected her from the sun. Since she had to ride like a man, the petticoat would have encumbered her legs, anyway.

The tracks were in places only a scrape of a horseshoe on a rock or a turned stone, but she had lived in the desert all her life and hunted with her father until his death, so she knew what to look for and what would have distracted her for no reason.

Now she sat in the shade of a roadside mesquite and took a sparing drink. Her face throbbed but the bandage was no longer wet with blood, and she debated soaking it with water, but decided it was more valuable to keep herself and the horse going.

She knew she could not be too far from Mesquite Springs, a tank fed by a spring from above. It was reputed to be hard to find, but she knew what to look for, and already she had seen two or three bees flying past her. Bees need a lot of water, and never live far from it, so the spring must be somewhere near.

'Trouble is,' she told the horse, 'I don't know exactly where, and them owlhoots may be there already. They surely ain't a-raisin' no dust.'

The horse flicked its ears at her but had nothing to contribute to the conversation.

The men who were looking for her as eagerly as she was looking for Karl and Pinkerton, on the other hand, were raising some dust, and it was bothering Obadiah. He slowed the pace of their march, and then slowed it again.

The dust was not by any means a cloud, but an experienced desert man would be able to see it if he looked hard enough and the men they were following were experienced desert men, all right. They were used to being followed, too, and they would be watching their back-trail like turkey buzzards on the hunt. They wouldn't miss the dust, though they might not realize it was raised by men hunting them.

He shook his head: 'The guilty flee where not man pursueth,' he murmured to himself. 'This pair is as guilty as all get out. They see dust, they'll think it's the posse. No way round that.'

He was badly torn. He wanted to catch up with Annie before she got herself into the hands of the outlaws, but he did not want the outlaws to know he was this close behind them.

Tomas's fine-chiselled nostrils had been smelling dust for a couple of miles now, and it would most likely be either from the fugitives or from Annie, who was, if he was interpreting the signs right, somewhere between pursuers and pursued.

CHAPTER NINE

Up ahead, two worried men lay on the reverse side of a rock ridge and scoured the landscape ahead.

'Nothing,' Karl said bitterly. 'No trees, no birds, nothing. You certain sure you heard of a tank here?'

Pinkerton was just as disappointed, but less surprised. He had heard of the Mesquite tank from a Mexican cattle-herder, knew it was in the Painted Desert around thirty miles south of Painted Rock, and knew it would water themselves and their horses. He threw a glance over his shoulder at the horses and was privately aghast at how bad they looked.

They stood, ground hitched, at the bottom of the short slope that led up to the little ridge. They stood with heads drooping and one occasionally scratched at the ground with a hoof as though he was trying to find water.

They were having about as much luck as their riders, which was none at all. The brothers had been searching for the tank for the last hour, and so far had not seen a sign.

'I said you got any ideas?' Karl repeated. He had chosen Pink as his companion on the escape from the jail because the man was the best shot of all the brothers, was brave, unlike Lemuel and cool-headed, unlike Donny. He had forgotten that the man was also as cold as a fish, and as chatty as a rock.

Pinkerton shook his head. 'Man told me there was a tank here, fed by a spring from above. That means it has to have a rock hanging over it, and the water has to come down from somewhere, so it must be at the foot of a hill. Me, I don't see no hills, so it can't be here.'

He was wrong, though. There was no hill, but there was a scarp slope, and they were sitting on top of it. From their side, it was a long and gentle slope upwards from the desert floor, and they had not noticed the climb. In front of them, only a little way in front, the land dropped sharply away and provided a respectable cliff. The spring was at the base of it. But from where they were lying, they could not see the drop-off, and in front of them was what looked like a gentle slope.

The water was invisible to them, but so were the Indians.

It was a small group of Indians, Hopi desert dwellers from the mesas to the west, and they had been hunting a long way out of their territory, where the game was currently poor.

They had been successful, and had made several kills, the meat from which was packed on their spare horse. They had a spare because one of their number had been killed during the hunt, and they had buried his body where he had fallen. The ceremonies which were required by their religion had been observed, and though they were unhappy about leaving him in alien territory, it would have been an uncomfortable and smelly journey to take him back to the mesas where his people had their homes.

The meat from their kills had been salted to make sure it kept on the journey, until it could be smoked and dried back home, but preserving it had meant using up all the salt they had. As one man pointed out, it was better to have live Hopis because they could eat the salted meat than dead ones because they had used to salt to preserve the dead.

Anyway, if they had taken him home instead of the meat they had gone forth to find, they would be bringing death to the mesa instead of life.

The decision was made, and they were filling their water gourds and pots for the remainder of the return journey. Two of the warriors were guarding the animals and the meat. Both were armed with bows and arrows. The group had no firearms.

None of this was known to the Driscoll brothers. They were not even aware of the presence of the Indians below them, or the lifesaving water which ran cool and clear there.

Until both groups were on the move.

The Driscolls disgustedly abandoned their vantage

point, and made their way downhill to their horses. Neither man wanted to admit it, but they were more worried about their mounts than they showed.

Out in the desert, a horse was life. Keep him fed and watered and he would take them anywhere they wanted. Let him thirst and he would very soon die. When he died it was just a matter of time until his rider did the same.

As they rode it became obvious that they were coming down from a height to a lower level, and they began to hope that, after all, they might find water.

They were on their way down to the desert when they saw the Indians come out along the base of the cliff. There were the two scouts, moving cautiously, followed by the little line of horses and the loaded packhorse.

From this distance they could not tell what tribe the Indians belonged to, and they did not much care. There were six warriors. Only a would-be suicide took on six armed Indians, and the Driscolls stayed in cover until the small cavalcade rode out into the desert, heading south and west, and the dust trail had settled. Then they rode down to where they had seen the Indians emerge, and discovered the water.

They were so relieved to find their water that they did not notice the tiny cascade of stones which slid down the scarp, raising a small dust trail which settled quickly.

Above them on the hill, reins tied to her wrist,

Annie watched where they went and then looked back along her own back-trail. An hour ago she had seen dust back there, and it had been there again twenty minutes later. She hoped fervently that it was old Obadiah with a posse.

Obadiah reined in and examined the tracks again. Now he was worried. The tracks he had been following diverged here, the brothers' horses going on up the slope to where he knew they would find their direction cut off, so if they had gone up, they would have to come down again.

But the girl's horse had carried on along the trail, apparently missing the turn-off, so he was worried that she had overrun the outlaws she was following and would be detected and caught. The thought made him deeply uneasy, and he could see Tomas's reasoning running on the same line.

Obadiah and Tomas decided to follow the girl, and carried on along the old trail. Paulus, who did not know the area, wisely followed where they led. But his rifle was across his knees and his right hand rarely left the loading lever.

So they came across the trail of the Hopi hunting party first.

Tomas's face darkened when he saw them.

'Unshod ponies,' said Obadiah, heavily. 'Apaches? Will they head her off?'

But ponies' hoofprints do not wear war paint, and not even Tomas could say who was riding on their backs. Like the old frontiersman, he naturally thought of Apaches this far over. Navajo territory and the Canyon de Chelly homelands were away to the west. So, too, were the Hopi mesas.

They ruled out anything but Apaches, and rode with extra care.

Securely tucked behind her rock, Annie whetted her borrowed knife and watched the trail. She had watered her horse from the water bottle, and drunk deeply herself. If the outlaws left the tank soon she could fill the bottle there. If they stayed by the water for the night, which was coming on fast, she would wait out here, where she could see them return to the trail, and identify the makers of the faint dust cloud when they came down from the north. She was quite pleased with her plan.

But her horse was not. He had welcomed the two scanty drinks he had been given so far, but the heat of the desert and the dust had dried his mouth almost as soon as it had been wetted. He could smell the water down under the cliff which was tantalizingly close at hand, and he desperately wanted to plunge his muzzle into it and drink his fill.

He jerked his head with agitation, and his trailing rein was pulled out from the rock Annie had put on it. Normally, having the loose rein trailing down to the ground served to ground hitch a Western horse, once he was trained to it, but this horse was thirsty

113

and there was water and, his nostrils told him, other horses close by.

Head free, he raised his muzzle and whinnied loudly and piercingly to the evening sky. He was answered instantly from just under the hill and the temptation became intolerable. He raised his head and trotted round until he came to where the splashing of water told him there was plenty to drink.

Pinkerton heard him coming and crouched behind a rock near the little waterfall, his Winchester ready to fire. When the horse, saddled but unridden, came into view he straightened up cautiously, suspecting a trap. When he realized that the horse was alone he followed its path with narrowed eyes to the shoulder of the hill, then grabbed at the reins of his own mount and vaulted into the saddle.

The drink of water had revived the mount magically, and the horse went off obediently at a fast clip which brought him to the shoulder of the hill just as Anne, who had been trying to catch the horse, arrived at the other side of it, heard the hoofs approaching and stepped out, relieved, to grab for his bridle.

When she saw it was Pinkerton she tried to throw herself back behind the rock, but the outlaw was quicker. He drove his mount between her and the rock, reached down and grabbed at her burnoose.

The tightly wound cloth acted as a noose, and she was dragged, kicking and hanging on to the cloth, down the slope to the spring. Her horse, still thirsty, was already there; it seemed to be trying to drink the desert dry.

Pink dropped her at Karl's feet, where she half-lay, hoarsely dragging in breath after breath.

'Looky what I've found,' Pink said, dropping from his saddle and dragging Annie towards the spring. He threw the struggling girl on to the ground and began to unwind her head covering. When he realized who she was he sat back on his heels and whistled.

'Well, I'll be a monkey's uncle!' he said, softly. 'Who in the name of all that's holy did that to you, girl?'

Even in the fading light, her face was a mess. The split skin, though the wound was not deep, had bled profusely, and soaked the material she had wound round it. The bruising over her cheekbone was spectacular, and one side of her face had swelled to almost twice its normal size. With the dust of the desert caked over it, the wounded cheek looked gruesome.

She had been a beautiful girl with spectacular bone structure, and now she looked grotesque.

'Who the hell did this to you, girl?' Pinkerton repeated. Her eyes flickered towards Karl. Pink followed the look and whistled. 'Didn't think even you was capable of this kind of thing, brother mine.'

He stood up and gestured at the little pond under the tumbling rill from the cliff face.

'Clean yourself up, girl, and don't even think of

running away. I can pick out your eyes at a hundred yards and you wouldn't get half that far.'

He scavenged around the waterside, and gathered enough kindling and sticks to make a handful of fire. Once he had the flames going, he threw the coffee pot at the girl and snapped: 'Fill it!'

Still holding the side of her face, she did as she was told and brought the pot back to the fire. Her eyes avoided Karl the whole time, and she responded only to Pinkerton. Karl, who was himself secretly impressed by the damage one smack with a pistol had done, sat on a rock near the fire and rolled himself a smoke. He took his time over it, making the paper into a little trough, tapping the tobacco sack to fill it, and lastly rolling the smoke.

He twisted one end to keep the tobacco in, put the other between his lips and lighted it with a flaming twig from the fire. The blue smoke in the gathering dark looked almost luminous as it drifted across the fire.

Pink pulled a pan and some bacon from his saddle-bag and threw it to Annie. She caught it clumsily, and without needing to be told, put it on the fire. The bacon she threw back.

'You cut it. I don't have a knife,'she snapped. She deliberately avoided looking pleased, though she was encouraged that he had not found the knife under her skirt. While he was dragging her down the hill she had been tempted to make a try for it, but with her head captured, she would have needed to stab upwards and unsighted to hurt him, and she had been half-blinded by the cloth round her head. Instead, she pushed the pommel down below her waistband, where it was more difficult to get at but not as obvious.

Pink laid the bacon on a rock and sliced off three thick rashers. These accounted for most of the meat, but he wanted them all to eat. He took flour from his saddle-bag, and mixed it with water from the spring to make campfire bread. He twisted the dough round a stick and hung it in the flames.

'Watch it!' he told the girl, and retreated to the rock where his brother leaned, smoking another coffin-nail cigarette.

'You do that?' he asked. Karl nodded. 'She riled me,' he said.

'You don't say,' said Pink, watching the girl as she mixed the coffee. He noted her calculating glance at the two of them as she wrapped the remains of her petticoat round the handle of the coffee pot and prepared to bring it to them.

'Hold it!' he snapped. 'Leave the pot where it is. I'll come get it.'

She looked crestfallen, but stepped back from the fire obediently enough. He pulled a glove on to his left hand, and took the pot back to the rock. Karl found the coffee cups.

Both of them watched her as she slapped the bacon into the skillet and put it back on the fire.

But the bacon had only just started to spit on the

117

little fire when a deep, rumbling growl came from the darkness beyond the circle of firelight. Both men grabbed for their rifles and stood up.

'What in tarnation's name is that?' hissed Pink. He was genuinely shocked at the closeness of the sound. It came from a deep chest, buried in a big creature and the only really big animal in these parts was a bear.

'Grizzly,' the girl said carelessly. 'You get them round here, time to time. We get 'em in town when they're hungry. He's thirsty and you're sitting on his water.'

She poked at the bacon with a stem of mesquite. It spat angrily, and the flames flared. The smell got stronger and, outside the firelight, the bear rumbled again.

Pink began to stuff the things back into his saddle-bag. Karl watched him, amused.

'You ain't afeered of a little ol' bear, are you, brother? Not a man as fast with a gun as you are?'

'Better than beating on women,' Pink said tersely, and went on packing the few things into his saddle-bag. He was aware out of the corner of his eye that Karl was reacting angrily to the sneer, and smiled to himself. An angry man was a hasty man, and it could be fatal to act hasty with Pinkerton Driscoll. He slipped the thong off the hammer of his Colt and watched Karl carefully.

His brother glanced around. There was a third growl from out beyond the firelight, and it sounded closer in.

'He's getting impatient,' said the girl nervously. 'You fixing to stay here? I don't want to be here when that grizzly gets to wondering who's making the coffee tonight. No, sir, I do mortally want to be someplace else.'

Karl reached over and took the pan from her. It was hot and he swore and dropped it, sending the bacon into the sand. Pink watched him carefully, his hand hanging down by his hip. It was almost touching the butt of his Colt, and Pink knew that no matter what Karl did, Pink could get his shot off first.

The bear growled again, this time a long, threatening angry sound, and Anne grabbed for the saddle horn. As both brothers looked towards her, and Karl started to protest, she swung herself into the saddle and kicked back with her heels.

The horse, already nervous about the growling from the darkness, went off like a rocket into the darkness. Pink tried to grab at her as she went past, but she was gone before he could get a firm hold.

Karl shouted at him, and the bear charged.

It was not a grizzly bear but a black bear.

He was big, nearly six feet, and in the flickering light from the fire he looked much bigger. From the point of view of the outlaw brothers, he was Hell come to breakfast. All they could see was a huge, shapeless black mass with a gaping red maw and teeth enough for a crocodile. And he was moving fast.

Pink's horse swapped end for end as the bear went

past him, and nearly threw his rider. Karl's, ground hitched, squealed like a hurt child and made one last despairing try at a leap out of the bear's path, but he was too late. The bear raked him with its claws as it went past, and laid open its stomach like a surgeon's stroke.

Karl grabbed for Pink's arm and was swept up behind him on the horse's rump, The mount in its turn went off at frightening speed. The bear, distracted by the horse's screaming and the smell of blood, swerved from the water hole and killed the screaming animal. Then, grumpily, it settled down to feed.

Around the water hole there fell a silence broken only by the sound of the bear's feeding and the steady trickle of water from the cliff.

It was very peaceful, and then, as the fire burned low, very dark. From the desert came the remote sound of a horse's hoofs, but in the end even they faded.

CHAPTER TEN

Obadiah Peabody hunkered down in the desert and struck a match on the seat of his tightly stretched pants. It flared on the third try and he examined the tracks he had been following and swore bitterly.

The match, burning down, singed his hand, and he swore again, wet his fingers and pinched it out. It took several seconds for his eyes to accustom themselves to the darkness again, during which few seconds he was effectively blind. He felt vulnerable and helpless in the darkness, and the feeling made him jumpy and short of temper.

'Well? What do you reckon?' said Paulus. Obadiah shrugged, forgetting the shrug was invisible in the darkness, then he remembered and said: 'We bin following the wrong tracks, that's what I reckon. Dunno how. This here trail's three mounts, and not Indians at that. There's a sight more people around here than there should be. Best wait for morning, and then we'll find her.'

Paulus swung down from his horse and waited for what came next. He was a solid, patient man, but this tracking in the darkness seemed uncanny to him. The desert was full of unexpected noises, some of which were only just within the range of his hearing, though he could not identify them. Then there were the tantalizing smells which rose in the night and could never be identified.

Lighting a match in the dead of night seemed insane to him, but he accepted that when Tomas and Obadiah agreed on something like this it was a raw necessity. Nevertheless, the flare of light in the dark could only attract unwelcome eyes, not all of which belonged to the creatures of the desert night.

Obadiah was just as jumpy, though it did not show in his behaviour. He had lit the match only as a very last resort, and it had proved pointless. The only thing it told him was that they had somehow lost the tracks. He swung back on to his horse, and stood in the stirrups to survey the silver and black landscape around them, plated by the moonlight and, to the naked eye, totally empty of life.

They had missed out at every point. First, they had overridden the girl's tracks and missed the point where she had turned off up the hill. He blamed his hurry to catch up with her for that.

Then they had been dismounted when her horse ran away and betrayed her to the outlaws at the waterfall. Obadiah had been sure she would remain in cover until the outlaws showed themselves, but the runaway horse had put paid to that possibility.

He was as startled as everybody else when the girl was captured, for it had happened way over to one side when he thought she must be straight ahead. So much for his skill as a tracker, he told himself for the umpteenth time and with bitterness. The girl had looped back on herself, and he had not known.

When she was captured by Pinkerton, he had seen only a struggling figure being towed along by what looked like a towel round its head, and he had not realized until too late that it must be Annie, by which time she had been pulled down into the little cove in the cliff where the spring had worn itself a basin.

The three hunters had to work their way through the thickening dusk to get a clear shot into the cove, by which time it was full dark. They saw the girl putting together a fire, saw her exchanges with her captors, and saw the coffee being made. They even got a tantalizing whiff of the bacon being fried.

Disaster struck when the bear shouldered its way into the scene. Obadiah could actually see its bulk between him and the little fire-lit tableau by the spring. When the bear made its charge and Annie and the loose horse vanished into the night, he knew exactly what had happened.

'Don't those guys know nothing?' he exploded into Paulus's ear.

'About what?' Paulus was confused. Mostly the two trackers communicated with one another in short grunts and gestures, which meant nothing to him. To avoid distracting them he swallowed his questions and kept his voice behind his teeth, as his mother used to say.

But if he was going to contribute to their hunt, he needed to know what they were doing.

'Don't never camp at a water hole,' Tomas told him. 'Everything that comes this way knows where it is, and most of them will certainly come to it for water. In the desert, you cannot avoid it. You must take your drink, water your horse, fill your canteen, yes, but then you move on. Stay where you are and everything in the desert will come to you.'

'Like a black bear?'

'And the rattlers, and the Gila monsters, and the coyotes – you seen a full grown desert coyote? They are almost as big as a wolf – and the wild cats and the lions, and the wolves of course.'

'And that is not even counting the men?'

'That is not counting the men, who are more dangerous than all of these things put together.'

So here they were in the darkened desert, having lost their quarry and her trail. They had no chance of picking up the trail again in the moonlit dark. Easy enough to see to ride their own horses: impossible to pick out the tracks they needed from the hundreds of shadows and silvered rocks.

They could not move without losing what little trail they had. So they loosened the girths and unsaddled the horses, and hunkered down in the rocks and sand to wait for morning.

By mutual consent Tomas took the first watch. Obadiah wrapped himself in a bundle of blankets and scruffy furs which smelled, and was asleep instantly, his long rifle lying by his bed, and his hand on the butt. Paulus unsaddled, wrapped himself in the horse blanket, laid his head on his saddle and dozed uncomfortably in the biting cold of the desert night.

To his surprise, he was awakened by a hand on his shoulder and a murmured caution. It was Obadiah leaning over him, blankets wrapped over his shoulders.

'Quiet. Horses coming,' the old man said. He spoke in a low voice because a sibilant whisper carries on the cold night air and sounds like nothing else.

Paulus pulled his Winchester out of the blanket. Thanks to his precaution, the barrel and movement were still warm, instead of nearly freezing from the cold.

His head was close to the ground, so he could hear, not too far away, the sound of horses' hoofs hitting the ground. He could not distinguish how many horses, but he knew there were more than one. It was not the girl they were tracking, then.

A rock nearby moved in the moonlight and he was swinging his rifle when he realized it was Tomas, covered in a blanket. The draped cloth turned him into merely another lump in the landscape when he kept still.

Within a couple of minutes he could see the

approaching horses. There were three of them. The first was ridden by a man with a serape over his shoulders and a wide brimmed, floppy hat. A Mexican, then. A long way north of where he should be. Behind him came a second figure slumped over the saddle horn, and made shapeless by a draped blanket. The third was a man in a bulky jacket, and wearing a cap. They picked their way carefully across the desert, the leader holding his rifle by the stock, with the butt resting on his thigh and the muzzle high over his head.

'Busy desert tonight, horse,' murmured Obadiah's voice in his ear, and he was startled to find the man all but leaning on his shoulder.

Before the passing horses were out of sight Tomas was on his feet, throwing his saddle over his horse's back. Obadiah was doing the same and Paulus found himself yet again trying to catch up with them and find out what they were doing and why.

'Where we going?' he hissed at the others as he caught the cinch and drew it tight.

'Didn't ye see who that was in the middle of them three, horse? That there was my granddaughter, and, man! was my purty little granddaughter in bad company! Them others was slave traders from the Borders. I been after them bad acters for years, now. They make Apaches look like Sunday school preachers. Killing them will make this sad old world a cleaner place. Mount up and we'll go get her,' Obadiah said, ducking under his horse's belly to grab

126

the saddle girth. He caught it just as the horse turned its head to snap at him, and smacked it on the nose with a heavy wooden stirrup.

'Cross-grained critter! Bad-tempered horse is worse'n a bad-tempered woman,' he told Paulus. The wagon master was busy saddling his own animal, but took time to say over his shoulder: 'Got bigger teeth, too,' and heard Tomas snigger.

Then they were off on the trail of the girl and her new captors.

'That there wench can get herself captured by more men than the Alamo,' muttered Obadiah as he dropped into line behind Tomas. Paulus shot a look at him and realized his grumpiness came from fear for his adopted granddaughter. It made the crusty old man a good deal more acceptable, somehow.

The direction of their travel put them in the shadow while the trio ahead were outlined against the moonlit sky. Unless they stopped and rode back to look, the three ahead would not know about the three behind, which was what Obadiah was counting on.

'How did they find her, and how did she let herself get took prisoner, horse?' he said to Paulus more than once. There was a rough edge to his voice which betrayed his anxiety, but Paulus had no answers for him and held his peace.

But there was an aura about the eastern sky which said night was ending, and once the sun was up their cover of darkness would be lifted. They needed to catch up with the girl and her new captors soon.

Obadiah slowed down and let the others catch up with him.

'Sun's coming up and we're going to lose the dark,' he said tersely. 'I reckon we got to hit them in the dawn with the sun behind us. I'll take the leader in the sombrero. Tom, boy, you take the tail-ender. OK, horse?'

Paulus, irritated, protested.

'How about me?'

'You? You're the pinch-hitter, horse. We miss, you hit.'

Paulus bowed his head and prayed for a clear shot. Then he raised it, and cocked the Winchester. Obadiah saw the gesture, realized what it meant and nodded. Paulus, he told himself, was a man to ride the river with.

But it did not work out that way. As the sun came up and they closed in from their chosen direction the whole situation changed.

Their quarry was clear enough, off to their side. Another five minutes and they would be in position to stage their ambush. But as they swung their horses to face back the way they had come, they realized that the quarry had disappeared.

Puzzled, Paulus looked around him, and found only empty desert. Where the three riders had been was just a little dust, but no horses.

Puzzled and wary, the three men spread out and

rode cautiously towards the last seen position of their quarry. They were within a hundred yards of the spot when the answer became clear.

Although the desert looked like an unbroken flat expanse broken by rocks and the occasional cactus, stunted yucca and ocotillo cactus, at this point there was a knife-slender slot in the ground. The tracks of the horses they were following led into it, in single file.

Following the line of the slot, Paulus realized that they were looking up one of the subtle rises that the desert concealed. The slot might be at ground height here, but as it dropped away, the ground rose gently so that within a few yards of the entrance, the canyon was already well over the height of a mounted man. He leaned forward and looked cautiously into its dark depths. It was just wide enough for a mounted man to pass, though he would have to lean sideways in the saddle as the canyon wall wiggled away in a series of crazy bends and sideways contortions.

'Slot canyon,' Obadiah muttered. He rose in his stirrups and looked all round the horizon with care.

'What you looking for?' asked Paulus. The old man shot him a glance.

'Rain clouds,' he said. 'These here slots are drains. Not just close by, but miles away. See them clouds over by the mesa there?'

Paulus could see them, looking harmless and fluffy in the distance. They were miles away, where the mountains began, and he said so.

'But when they drop their rain, there ain't no place for it go on them rocks, horse. Don't soak in, don't stay still. Has to go somewhere, so runs off to the lower ground. Like here.'

He pointed at a fan of alluvial sand which spread from the narrow slot and carried on for a surprisingly long way across the open desert. Clearly cut into it were the hoofprints of the three horses they were following. They led straight into the canyon mouth.

'They gone in, which is how we come to lose them. Trouble is, how long is it? Once we're in, there ain't no turning back. And if them clouds turn to rain have we got time to get out? Can you swim, horse?'

Paulus had been a sailor at one time in his life and, like a lot of sailors, had a horror of being washed overboard and left in the middle of the ocean watching his ship sail away from him ignorant of his fate. He had to admit he could not swim. He shook his head.

'Best thing, really. Try and swim if this fills up and all you do is make drowning last longer. You game?'

He had come this far, so he might as well go the length. In any case, Tomas was already guiding his horse into the entrance of the canyon, so Paulus fell into line behind him. Obadiah brought up the rear as tail-ender.

'Don't worry, horse,' he said with a grin when Paulus looked back at him. 'If you get swept down, I'll catch you!' His cackle sounded very hollow.

Now they were committed. As he realized that, the canyon brought to his ears, faint and remote like the growl of a roused wolf, a mutter of thunder.

CHAPTER ELEVEN

Within the walls of the canyon the cold of night was slow to dissipate, and Paulus was glad of his coat. He pulled the collar up around his ears and slipped his carbine back into the saddle boot. In this narrow, winding space it would be more of a danger to him than anybody else, and it could easily get jammed across the twisting slot and sweep him over his horse's rump. He drew the Colt from its holster and slipped it behind his belt buckle, where the butt was close to his hand though inside the front of the coat. With a quick grab he could bring it into action in a second.

Ahead of him he could see Tomas, bending this way and that to accommodate the wild twists of the canyon. The man seemed to be able to keep up a good pace despite the tight bends and weird shapes. The waterborne grit and pebbles had worn horizontal grooves in the canyon walls, and as he rode Paulus could see the fine sand caught in them; he noticed how even the gentlest of movement sent the powder-fine sand falling to the floor.

When he looked up he could occasionally see the remains of branches of desert plants, jammed in the tight twists of the canyon walls, and stripped of bark or outer skin by the sand and pebbles carried in the water. When he thought of what the same sandblasting could do to human flesh, his stomach lurched.

Tomas seemed to be gaining on him and in his hurry he scraped his leg against the side of the canyon. The sharp striations in the wall cut through his jeans like knives and drew blood, but he made no attempt to stop and examine the half-dozen tiny cuts. By now all he wanted was to be out at the end of this death trap and in the open desert again.

Also, a new sound was beginning to make its presence known. A growling rumble, far away as yet but growing with every yard they travelled.

'Hurry up, horse,' Obadiah growled behind him. 'We got to get out of here right smart! That ain't no cattle stampede you can hear.'

Careless of the walls and the soft sand underfoot, he pushed the horse and the mustang responded with such enthusiasm that he realized it was as nervous as he was.

The end came unexpectedly. They must have been in the slot for nearly half an hour when suddenly the roof began to open up again and sunlight fell on the walls. The light changed from a misty butter colour to a bright, hard yellow.

The floor lifted slightly, and the horse went up it like a monkey up a ladder. At the top Tomas was standing in his stirrups and peering through slitted eyes up the now open canyon. As Paulus came up out of the narrow cut, he gestured up the slope to the side.

'Up! Water comes!' he snapped and Paulus urged the horse up the steep rock-strewn slope to his right, and felt it throw itself up like a mountain goat. Fast as it was, Obadiah's big, awkward horse passed it and scrambled on to the shoulder of the pass. Tomas was there already, his horse standing on a kind of shelf only a few feet below the lip.

Even so, the wall of water which came round the bend ahead nearly caught them. It was carrying on its face a collection of debris which included old tree branches, a few cacti, and even stones which rattled along the walls, propelled by the water. On its crest a tree's remaining skeleton tossed broken, splintered arms which would have gutted a horse like a butcher's knife.

The whole flood, which was being compressed by the walls of the canyon as it travelled, gave off a sound like a racing locomotive, a roar and a rattle which was deafening.

Paulus dragged his eyes away from the brown flood, returning his pistol to its holster and fastening the thong over the hammer spur to make sure it stayed there. Then he leaned forward to draw his Winchester from the saddle boot, and as he worked the action to throw a cartridge into the chamber, the canyon wall near his head exploded and spat fragments over his cheek.

Without waiting, the horse leapt forward, stung by the gravel, and Paulus heard both Tomas's and Obadiah's guns bang out. There was a scream, and above the roar of the torrent he heard another shot.

He was bent over his horse's neck and looking back up the canyon to where the water was racing round a bend. In the water he saw a head racing downstream.

He had just time to grab at his lariat and throw the loop out over the water. It went beyond the floating head, but an arm came out of the water and grabbed it. The action of the flood wrapped the line round the arm, and only the fact that Paulus had automatically taken a double turn round the saddle horn prevented him being torn from the saddle. The horse, accustomed to taking the strain, straightened its front legs and sat back on its haunches, but even so he felt it quiver as the weight of the floating human hit the end of the line. The water built up around it instantly and the weight of the swimmer swung the line in to the canyon edge, where the speed of the water was slowed by the rocks.

Even so, it took all the strength of the horse and Paulus combined to drag the bedraggled wreck out of the flood and on to the edge of the canyon. As it lay there, blowing weakly, he saw that it was a woman.

As he hauled her upright and across the saddle of

his horse, more shots were rattling down the narrow canyon. He reckoned there could not be fewer than three shooters, and that they were all shooting at the bedraggled woman.

He grabbed her and pulled her against the side of the canyon, where they were sheltered by the over-hang of the lip. She was straining herself against the rock, and another shot tore stone chips from the shelf they were standing on. It hit a few feet out, in the middle of the shelf, and he realized that the shooter was unsighted by the edge of the canyon, and would have to shift position to get a clear shot at them.

His Winchester had fallen from his hand and was lying out near the edge of the shelf, beyond his reach. The woman he had rescued appeared to be trying to burrow into the rock wall, and her position put her well out of the line of fire, so he took his pistol in hand and threw himself in a roll across the ledge to the rifle.

As he did so, stone chips spat from the ledge near his head, and he could see the head of the shooter outlined against the morning sky as he levered his carbine to repeat the shot.

The Colt had a long barrel, Paulus was a good shot, and the sniper was close to the edge of the canyon, leaning closer to get a clear shot.

The Colt's soft .44 slug cut a groove through the stock of the sniper's rifle and took him under the chin, emerging, deformed and monstrous, at the back of his head. The big, floppy hat twitched as the bullet passed through it, and Paulus distinctly saw the blood fan momentarily over the exit wound. The rifle clattered down the rock and fell into the rushing water.

Clutching his own rifle, Paulus took a quick look along the rim before he threw himself back into cover, and saw the arm and shoulder of another marksman above the rim, a little further down the canyon. It was too far for him to rely on a lucky hit with his Colt, but even as he tried to get the Winchester into action, there was a much deeper boom from away to his right, and the arm and shoulder disappeared.

Safe back against the wall of the canyon, he peered along the stone shelf, and saw Obadiah feeding another cartridge into the long rifle. The old man was kneeling like a contender in a marksmanship contest, squatting back on one heel, with the other leg stretched in front of him. As Paulus watched he did a curious little hop sideways on his bent leg and put the rifle to his shoulder.

There was another of the deep reports, and a scream from above, and Obadiah stood up, reloading again. Further along the ledge Tomas emerged from behind a shoulder of rock, his horse's reins hooked over his arm and his own rifle half-raised as he surveyed the rim above them.

No target presented itself, and he relaxed without taking his eyes from the edge. Obadiah walked along towards him, surveying the opposite side of the canyon, but he rested his rifle butt down by his feet without firing.

'I reckoned there was three and we got three, horse,' he said, taking off his bandanna and wiping his neck. 'Good shooting, wagon master. Tricky angle if ever I seen one. Who's your friend?'

The woman Paulus had dragged from the flood was sitting in a soaking heap against the canyon wall, near his horse. Her bedraggled head was bent forward, and her hands lay helplessly empty in her lap. She had been wearing a white blouse and a long, dark skirt at some time in the past, but both had been sadly damaged by the flood, and now she sat barely covered by the rags. Paulus thought he had seen more women in disarray in the past twenty-four hours than he had seen in a year. He shrugged off his coat and dropped it in her lap.

She looked up at him through the tangled hair with empty eyes and, after a moment, made some attempt to pull the coat over her shoulders. Somewhere along the line she had been badly scraped by the rocks, and the scrapes were bloody. She pulled the coat over her shoulders and, under it, tore off the remains of her blouse, using them to wipe the scrapes. Then she shrugged the coat on.

She made no attempt to talk. He leaned down and pulled the hair back from her face to find she had been gagged with a leather thong. It was cutting into her cheeks. He pulled out his knife, slit the thong behind her head and she spat it out.

'*Gracias, señor,*' she said in a rusty croak, worked her mouth and spat into the rushing water.

Tomas, cradling his rifle, dropped to his haunches, and leaned over her.

'*Quien es? Qué pasa?*' he asked, and she instantly became more animated.

She was Inez, the wife of a Mexican ranch hand from north of the Canyon of the Colorado, she said. They had been bringing cattle south to sell to the Army at Fort Apache when they were attacked by what they at first thought must be Indians.

They? Who were 'they', she was asked.

A half-dozen hands and their boss, she said. They worked for a Señor Clifton, though her eyes flickered when she said it, and Paulus wondered briefly where and how Señor Clifton had acquired his herd. He decided it was a question best left unasked.

What was she doing with a trail herd? It was rare for the cowboys to have a woman with them, or even want one.

'I cook,' she said. But her eyes slid off to one side again when she said it, and Paulus took it to mean she had been taken along by the boss to keep his blankets warm at night. Rare, but not unheard of.

Where were the rest of her party now?

Dead, she said. She alone had been kept alive, and added to the others.

'Others? What others?'

There were six other women, she said. All young,

all stolen from the various little ranches and communities in and around the desert. Another had been found in the night when two of the men riding behind the main party had come across her almost by accident along their back trail.

She had a face wound but she was in good shape, so they had brought her along. But the two men were being followed, so they and another had turned back to get rid of the pursuers.

The story was not a particularly common one, but neither was it unheard of. Women stolen from the Arizona and New Mexico Territories fetched a high price in Mexico. Every now and again Paulus had heard of women raids, though the raiders were rare and even more rarely got as far north as the Canyon.

When the water came down the slot canyon the raiders were taken by surprise. There was chaos while they broke camp and salvaged their human merchandise, particularly since one of them had only just been brought in. During the chaos the Mexican girl broke away from her bonds and ran for freedom.

She had not counted on the speed of the rising water, and when she started out on the path along the canyon it caught her up and washed her away.

Which way did the fleeing slavers go? She shrugged and gestured up the canyon. Which way could they go? she asked. The flood closed the canyon. They had to go upstream.

How many of them? Maybe ten in all. Maybe more.

Taking away the three who had just been killed, that left at least seven. How many women? That she knew. There were seven, including her. Two were very young.

They mounted up and cautiously followed the line of the ledge along above the flood. At one point it dipped into the water and the horses were uneasy about entering the speeding stream, however shallow, but after a little persuasion they did it.

They had not gone far when they found a body. It was of a young girl, scarcely more than a child. Her throat had been cut, and a glance at the body told why. She had a broken ankle and could not run. Also it made her unsaleable on the market.

Obadiah looked at the young body for a long moment, then he pulled out his knife and all three men helped scrape a grave for her. It took half an hour and they piled rocks on her to try and keep the predators away. All the men were painfully aware that with every minute the slavers and their women were getting further away.

'Don't worry, horse,' Obadiah told them. 'We'll catch them before dark. I know where they're going: Dark Canyon. Makes good hideout but she's a pure-dee bitch as an escape route.'

'Could they escape?' Paulus asked. The old man shook his head.

'Not from me, horse. Not from me,' he said, and from the expression on his lined, granite-hard face Paulus knew he was right.

141

With the girl taking turns to ride double, they pushed on. The tracks told them where to go and they needed only one reason to follow them.

CHAPTER TWELVE

It took them all day to reach the shadowy slash in the desert wall which was the gateway to Dark Canyon, but both Obadiah and Tomas read the trail like a mission Bible. The slavers were good at concealing their trail, but the vengeful men were better at uncovering it, and the various tricks used held them up only a little.

'Helps because I reckon I know where they're heading, horse,' Obadiah grunted when Paulus asked him, after watching with awe while the old man cast a large semicircle from a point where the tracks apparently vanished altogether. He picked up the real track within minutes. 'Every time they lays a false trail, I reckon I know where they bound to pop up next, and dang me if they ain't right there.'

Obadiah paused for a moment, then: 'Of course, if they manage to cross another trail in this kind of country, that could throw me for a while. Ain't tracking individual animals in this. They leave a scrape, turn over a stone, that's all.

'Soft ground, now that's different. You can read the horses theirselves, tell which one's lame, which one's nervous, and of what. Some pull a bit to the right or left. Some shy at shadows. Trailed one once had been scared by a rattler when he was a colt. Wouldn't go within ten foot of a big rock, where there might be a snake. That's how I knew him when I caught up with him.'

He took a plug of tobacco from his breast pocket, sliced a chew from it and offered it to Paulus. The wagon master shook his head.

'Ain't one of my vices, friend,' he said, and the old trapper shot him a look as sharp as a gimlet.

'Baccy settles a man's stomach and calms his passions, horse,' he said. 'Don't call that much of a vice, my own self. But you do what you think is fittin' for a man.'

He checked the load in his long rifle completely unnecessarily, winked, and pointed.

'Them women-stealers is snugging down for the night right there, and that is right where we'll bury them, horse. I want them girls out and I want them out without one hair on their heads so much as bruised, and if one more o' them maidens is hurt, I'm going to build me a slow fire, and roast me some evil men.'

Paulus swallowed hard, but he had seen the expression on Obadiah's face when they found the body of the girl with the broken ankle, and he did not for one second doubt his sincerity.

144

*

They rode up to the canyon mouth in extended open order, with Paulus on the right hand, Obadiah in the middle and Tomas on the left. In the short dusk they must have looked like dark ghosts drifting in from the desert, and for just one second Paulus found himself wondering whether they were entirely alone.

He shook himself and drew the Winchester from its boot as the three converged on the canyon entrance. Whatever they had to fear, it was totally real and solid, and if it gave him the thin end of half a chance, he wanted to shoot large holes in it.

The girl, now shivering in Paulus's coat, clung to his back. She had recovered a lot of her confidence on the ride, but now that they were within striking distance of the slavers once again, she was quivering like a kitten. He could hear the breath hissing between her teeth by his ear.

The darkness of the canyon was daunting at first. But they were not more than a few hundred yards down the track when Paulus was aware of a lifting of the blackness ahead, a gentle glow against which the rocks ahead began to stand out.

Obadiah reined in and let Paulus catch up with him.

'There they are,' he breathed into the wagon master's ear.

Paulus was tense. 'No sentries?'

145

Tomas appeared next to them, a ghost in the dark of the canyon.

'Not now,' he said. 'Six men left. One sentry other side fire. The women are against the canyon wall under an overhang. They are tethered and cannot run. We must go and get her.'

Paulus squinted towards him in the dark. 'Her?'

'All of them, of course!' But it was obvious whom he really meant. In Tomas passion ran deep and strong.

They walked the horses as close to the glow of the fire as they dared and then went forward on foot, leaving them tied to a scrubby bush.

'Something goes wrong, they can soon pull that up,' Paulus protested, then wanted to kick himself for missing the fact that the animals could escape rather than starve. Neither of the other men pointed it out, though whether from contempt at his missing the obvious or just simple tact he could not work out.

Obadiah halted them a little back from the camp-site, and held a short conference with Tomas.

'I'll go round this side, and you go round that. Girl, you stay here, with the horses,' he said confusingly, and then had to explain to both men what he was talking about. Obadiah himself was to approach the canyon side of the fire, and Tomas the cliff side since he was more agile and could deal with the climbing involved better than the old man.

Paulus opened his mouth to protest that he too was agile, but looked at the expression on Tomas's face in the flickering red gloom, and shut it again. Suddenly he felt a twinge of something near pity for the lone sentry out there. His death would not be an easy one.

'Why not just creep up on the fire and shoot them there?' he asked Obadiah as Tomas pulled one of his silent and sudden disappearing acts. Obadiah hunkered down to wait, rifle held between his knees.

'On account of they ain't round the fire and we need to know where they're at,' the old man explained softly.

'Not by the fire?'

'That there fire's the only light in this here canyon, maybe in this here desert,' he was told. 'If you was figuring on staying alive, would you be sitting in front of it, all nicely outlined for target practice? And killing your night vision, too? Them slavers may be as cuddlesome as tarantulas, but they ain't stupid.'

'How do you know they ain't? Sounds a pretty evil calling to me.'

'Evil I grant you. I know they ain't stupid on account of they're still alive and in business. Slavers ain't loved nowhere in the world that I know of. If they're alive, they're either right clever or they're damn lucky . . .'

From the darkness at the other side of the fire's glow there arose a scream so awful, so racked with agony and horror, that Paulus almost dropped his gun.

'. . . and their luck just plumb run out. That was

147

the other sentry,' said Obadiah. 'Watch for muzzle flashes and shoot back.'

As he spoke, guns began to fire in the darkness of the canyon, and Paulus fired back at them. He had shot only two rounds when the old man laid a hand on his.

'Which shoulder do you shoot from?' said Obadiah.

'My right.'

'Likely they do, too. Shoot a mite to the left of the flash and you got more chance. And move after each shot. They can pull that trick, too.'

Paulus had been reckoned a crack shot in his cavalry unit. But he learned more in the next few minutes than he had in the army during the whole of the war. He got a scream after his third shot, and that rifle fell silent. Pleased, he turned to find another, and was disappointed. The opposition was over.

Cautiously, he called out, then slid out from his latest hiding-place and made his way towards the fire.

As he went he heard a girl's voice screaming: 'No! No! Help us, help us!' and then came a terrible hoarse scream of agony, and the sound of weeping.

Horrified, he ran forwards, hurdling the fire, and found himself standing over a twitching, moaning body which appeared to be trying to cram its intestines back into its belly cavity with reeking hands. Beyond, turned red by the flames, a group of girls was crouching against the canyon wall. In front of them, Tomas was untying Annie's hands.

Paulus instinctively began to bend over the terribly injured man, but Tomas snapped: 'Leave him. He is dying.'

'But we could do something—'

'You would prefer to see him over a slow fire? We do not have much time, but we can try it if you like.'

Paulus shook his head, revolted.

'Leave him, then. It will take him a while, but he will die in the end. He was the one who killed the little one when she broke her leg. He was going to kill my Annie.'

Paulus understood, but he was still revolted.

'What are you going to do with them, then?'

'Do? Nothing. They are dead, all but him.'

'We could bury them.'

There was a silence, broken only, suddenly, by a coyote's mournful call, out in the desert.

'Why?' Tomas jerked his head to indicate the unseen coyote. 'He has a right to eat, too. Leave them. Tonight, the desert feeds well.'

'But he is not dead. We cannot leave him to the coyotes!'

'He left the little girl with the broken ankle to the coyotes. He would have left all of these women to the coyotes. He chose his bed. Leave him to lie in it.'

'But he is still alive. We cannot just leave him!'

Tomas shrugged. 'Have it your way, then.' He drew his pistol and blew the man's brains out, carefully reloading the chamber before he put the gun away.

*

As he released the other girls, none of them out of their teens, Paulus found time to resign himself to the brutal reasoning of the gunsmith. The girls had not been raped because their value would have been damaged as merchandise, but they had been brutally treated, and every one of them had been terrified. They flinched from his hands as he cut their bonds, and would not allow him to chafe their swollen wrists.

Paulus was a tough, hard man who had fought bravely through one of the most vicious wars of his time, but the treatment of these girls sickened him. Like most Western men he had been raised to respect women and, in his own way, to treat them gently. He had married for love and never regretted his choice, and to see young girls so terrified by their treatment that one of them was actually sick when he touched her aroused in him a smouldering rage which needed release.

He helped Obadiah stamp out the fire and scatter the ashes. Then he washed the girls' lacerated wrists in the unnameable spirits they found in a clay flask, and poured the rest away. He gathered the slavers' weapons to prevent the Indians finding them and Tomas wrapped the usable ones in a blanket and tied it tightly with a rope, and slung it on one of the captured horses. The worn and damaged weapons he smashed over a rock.

'Apaches are already dangerous without leaving arms for them,' he grunted. 'My mother's people do well enough with bows and arrows.'

The wink he shot at Paulus was just visible in the growing light.

The dawn was already painting the eastern sky a lemon shade by the time all was done, and Obadiah and Tomas had finished, searching the corpses. They laid them out in a line on their campsite and counted to make sure the number of corpses corresponded with the number of horses, then linked the mounts up in a line and set out into the desert.

CHAPTER THIRTEEN

Karl was beginning to worry about Pink. The brothers had been sharing the single horse for over twenty-four hours now, and their progress was slow. Trying to ride it double for any length of time was plainly out. They were both big men and the animal, though game, was becoming more and more distressed in the heat.

In their flight from the bear they had lost their water bag and when the girl had ridden off on their horse, they lost half their provisions, too. Now they had one canteen of water, and the contents of Pinkerton's saddle-bags.

They gave water to the horse, though it was nowhere near what the animal needed in these conditions, and drank some themselves. They ate bacon fried in the skillet, and it made them more thirsty. At this point Karl caught his brother looking at him with a calculating gleam in his eye.

There was no real love between the two brothers,

for they had been raised in a home without love, where the normal conversation was conducted in shouts and the normal human contact was a kick or a blow. Even in that hateful environment, Pink had been a misfit, an island of watchful, passionless still-ness surrounded by a sea of turmoil, rage and spite.

Now, he was calculating how long half a canteen of water would last two thirsty men and how very much longer it would last just one, and his conclusions were not hard to read.

They were already having to spell the horse, one of them riding and the other walking alongside, hold-ing the stirrup. Soon, it would occur to Pink that the horse would go twice as far with only one rider, and that it was, after all, his horse. Karl had some time previously come to this conclusion and the thought that his brother would sooner or later do the same was making him tense and watchful.

They spent the night in a cold camp, with neither brother willing to close his eyes first, and as a result they both slept badly. Desert nights are cold, and Pink did not offer to share his blankets, while Karl, after a careful look at his brother, did not push the matter, settling instead for the saddle blanket.

Both slept fitfully and were awakened before dawn by a barrage of firing off to the east. They did not, of course, know it, but it was the sound of three venge-ful men catching up with the slave traders and making sure they had traded their last slaves.

However, where there was firing there were usually

casualties, and dead riders meant spare horses. Their need was great, so they mounted double one last time and headed in the direction of the firing.

Travelling with a number of women and a small herd of horses meant that Obadiah, Tomas and Paulus were vulnerable and a tempting target for any bad men who happened to be ranging the desert – and an irresistible one for a wandering Indian, so the little party was heading for home and safety with both caution and speed, sticking to low ground when they could to avoid being skylined.

Tomas refused to be separated from Annie, so he rode with the women and the horses, while Obadiah scouted ahead and Paulus brought up the rear, with his Winchester resting across his knees and his eyes peeled for trouble as they never had been in his life before.

The other two men might be untiring – they certainly looked it – but they had been even busier than he the night before and human flesh would take only so much, so it was up to him to do his very best to hold up his end of the work. In any case, he was particularly keen to come face to face with the bandits who had seen fit to kidnap Betty.

In the event, he did the opposite.

Karl and Pinkerton saw the dust raised by the main party led by Tomas, who had taken to a low narrow valley. They correctly interpreted it as having been raised by several horses, and dropped in behind it to scout it and make sure the riders of those horses were not a threat to them.

They missed the much smaller dust trail raised by Paulus, or thought it part of the larger cloud which had not yet subsided, so they were between Paulus and the girls' party, and were unaware of Paulus's presence. Eyes focused on the larger, more tempting target ahead, they closed in on their prey, guns ready for trouble, hungry for loot and desperate for horses and water.

Paulus, however, did not miss their trail. He saw it come out of an arroyo and fall in behind Tomas and the girls, correctly assessed that the tracks meant trouble, on the principle that friendly travellers made their presence known in the desert, and eased back the hammer on the Winchester as he urged his horse to catch up with the new interlopers.

So that when Karl and Pinkerton closed in on Tomas and the girls, they were already sandwiched between men who were hunting them down.

Pinkerton eased the horse round a pile of rocks and cactus and found himself just behind the string of horses, which was following a group of young women and a single male rider along the draw. He could hardly believe his luck.

Karl, pistol drawn, dropped from the horse's rump and ran up the side of the draw so as to split the rider's point of aim, and whistled shrilly. Tomas, who had heard the approaching horse, but mistaken it for Paulus'a mount, which he thought was catching up, looked over his shoulder, saw his mistake, and swung

155

his horse to put himself between Annie and the levelled gun.

The kidnapped girls, already panicked by the appearance of two men with guns, screamed and, milling around, spoiling the aim of both Karl and Tomas.

Pink had never seen Tomas before, but he had seen Anne, and realized that she would identify him, which would cause trouble, no matter who the man with her might be. He stood in his stirrups, levering his Winchester, and threw a shot at her.

It missed, but the sound of the shot started the captured horses milling around, and his next shot hit one of them. It started screaming.

The dust raised by the horses was thick and he was peering for his next shot when Paulus came round the bend of the draw, holding his Winchester like a horse pistol, his horse galloping belly-down.

Paulus might be a learner so far as Obadiah and Tomas were concerned, but he knew what he was doing as a cavalry marksman, and he did it. His first shot went through Pinkerton's chest from under the shoulder blade and came out through his breast-bone, the big soft slow moving slug taking most of the bone with it. Annie said afterwards that she thought his chest had exploded,

His body was knocked forwards over his saddle horn, and the rifle he had been holding stopped the exiting bullet with its loading plate, which was smashed out of the weapon into a tangled mess.

Karl, halfway up the side of the draw, found he had nowhere to go. The bank ahead of him curved over like a breaking wave, and he was encumbered by his pistol when he tried to jump and catch it to drag himself up.

Tomas, standing in his stirrups, was shooting from the shoulder but his horse was jostled by the others in the string, which were plunging wildly all around him, and he was missing and cursing steadily.

Obadiah, however, had none of these drawbacks. At the first shot, he had whirled his horse on its haunches, and sent it hammering back the way it had come. He skidded round a bend in the draw to see what was happening ahead of him, hauled the ugly horse to a standstill and hit the dirt on one knee.

The rifle barrel dropped into his palm. His thumb automatically flicked back the cock, and the foresight drifted into line with Karl's forehead. The slug was on its way.

In the same second Tomas's horse hit the ground with both forefeet at once. The impact jolted his finger, firing his Winchester.

Karl's head exploded at the same instant that Tomas's slug entered his heart, and the two men who killed him never stopped arguing about whose shot had actually taken his life.

CHAPTER FOURTEEN

At a loss as to what to do with the kidnapped women, whose families had largely been slaughtered when they were captured, the townsfolk of Painted Rock first offered them homes in the community, which two of them accepted.

One – Inez – joined the Paulus family on its way to California, and there found a husband who did not beat her often or badly, and settled to raising chubby children and chickens.

The remaining three girls Paulus delivered to the authorities at Fort Apache when he passed through, along with his report about the slave traders and the fate of the Driscoll brothers.

'They get a fair trial?' asked the commanding officer, whose main concern at that time was a man called Cochise, who had disappeared into the mountains near Apache Pass, whence he proceeded to

158

become an ever-present nightmare.

'Certainly did,' Obadiah told him with a perfectly straight face. 'Me, I believes in the rule o' law. Leastways, they're all planted now.'

The commanding officer shot him a look which conveyed perfect understanding.

'Good,' he said. 'Posse chasing them from Hardwick got down as far as Lava Butte before they turned back. I'll let the sheriff know they're dead. Cheer him up. How's the hunting down the Salt, these days?'

They spent an agreeable half-hour over a glass of whiskey that, for once, had not been made locally and as a result did not contain rattlesnake heads for bite and a dead rat for body. The memory of the Driscolls faded from their minds and from the Territory.

Paulus passed through Painted Rock some years later and was surprised to find how much the town had grown. There was a courthouse where the roads crossed, white-painted timber homes, several saloons, a post office and four churches with steeples and bells. In the main street was a large general store with a sign which said in appropriately large letters: DELGADO GENERAL STORE. GUNS SOLD AND REPAIRED.

He was greeted within with noisy delight by both Tomas and Annie and a horde of olive-skinned children in graduated sizes who never stopped talking.

Within minutes his bag had been retrieved from the
room he had rented at the new, smart Bon Ton Hotel
by two of the sons, and reinstalled in a neat, comfortable room with a big iron bed and a wash-stand.
There was a very long gun rack for a single weapon
over the window.

It was empty. But the oil stains on the wood spoke
of regular use.

'Yes, it's his room, but we haven't seen him this
year. I wonder if he's still alive, myself, but Tom says
we'd have heard,' Annie said when she saw him looking at it. 'Generally he winters here, so there's time
yet. He'll have spent the summer thinking up
another reason why his bullet hit Karl Driscoll first.'

Paulus shot her a sideways glance. 'Did it?'

She turned her extraordinarily beautiful face
towards him and he wondered yet again at the way
the scar – now a faint silvery line across the swell of
her cheek – somehow enhanced her good looks.

'What do you think?' she said, and was gone
before he could answer.

'I don't have to think. I know,' he said to the
closed door.

But he never told her it was her husband whose
accidental shot had hit her would-be murderer
before her adoptive father's aimed bullet. He was
pretty certain she knew, anyway, but enjoyed the
argument over which of the men she held most dear
had saved her life.